FROM THIS DAY FORWARD

JEANNE TOMPKINS

Copyright © 2022 by Jeanne Tompkins

All rights reserved. This book or any portion thereof may not be reproduced or transmitted in any form or manner, electronic or mechanical, including photocopying, recording, or by any information storage or retrieval system, without the express written permission of the copyright owner except for the use of brief quotations in a book review or other noncommercial uses permitted by copyright law.

Printed in the United States of America

Library of Congress Control Number:	2022913671
ISBN: Softcover	979-8-88622-465-8
eBook	979-8-88622-466-5
Hardcover	979-8-88622-470-2

Republished by: PageTurner Press and Media LLC
Publication Date: 07/27/2022

To order copies of this book, contact:

PageTurner Press and Media
Phone: 1-888-447-9651
info@pageturner.us
www.pageturner.us

FROM THIS DAY
FORWARD

This book is dedicated to the carers of St Bede's. Without their wonderful care and kindness, I could no longer continue my independent lifestyle.

To Chris, he spent a great deal of his spare time keeping my computer up to scratch, without his help I don't think this book would ever be completed.

My grateful thanks to you all who have kept me going with their gentle encouragement; and finally Joe Bell for his infinite patience. Joe, we have made it!

CHAPTER 1

WEDNESDAY NOVEMBER 25TH 1998.

Kate awoke with a start, picking up her book from the floor she apologised to the passenger sitting next to her. Looking at her watch there was still another thirty minutes before the need to make sure she was looking presentable prior to landing.

How she hated late evening arrivals, fortunately she had only one piece of hand luggage and a small overnight bag, so she wouldn't have to stand forever in a queue waiting at the carousel.

Harvey Rutherford-Harris had arranged to meet the incoming plane, and had assured her his parents were looking forward to her joining them for Thanksgiving.

Harvey had insisted she would just love it. "Our family is much the same as yours although we also have my paternal grandparents living with us on a semi permanent basis."

As she strode through the airport arrivals, more than one set of male eyes followed her progress. Katherine Elizabeth McKenzie was well worth a second look. A little above average height, her skin a delicate shade of very pale peach, her face a perfect oval with sloe dark eyes under delicately arched black eyebrows. Her dark hair was tucked up inside a Russian style white fur hat.

Harvey catching sight of her in the concourse strode to meet her, taking her overnight bag from her he placed his other hand under her elbow, to guide this very attractive lady to his car.

Once they were seated inside out of the cold, he turned her face towards him giving her a chased kiss on the cheek.

"Good flight Kate, we'll be home in about forty minutes. My mother is so excited you have finally accepted an invitation to join us for Thanksgiving."

Kate had been invited to the Rutherford-Harris home several times over the past few years, how many years? Too many to remember, she had always made a gracious excuse why she was unable to accept, but this time Harvey said his family wished to reciprocate the hospitality the McKenzie family had shown to their son whilst attending one of the McKenzie weddings.

What they couldn't have known; Kate had asked Harvey to come as her guest, not because he was more than a dear friend, but to prevent any member of her family to try and fit her up with Jamie *Tallington*. She had drawn a line under that at Sebastian's wedding.

For a time she was close to Dr Charles Blossom, Professor of Botany, Lecturer at Cambridge University. They still corresponded but he had been in the Far East for almost the best part of the last three years, so Kate was once again waiting for something or someone to kick start her life again.

As she stepped out of the car into the cold clear air of New England her thoughts turned to home. Pipers Gate, the McKenzie family home, the air would feel and smell much the same as this but it would be home. In that single moment she felt a longing to return back to her family, to join in the preparations for the coming festive season.

"When this is over I'm going home." Harvey coming round to assist her from the car overheard Kate's remark.

"You're going home, when?"

"Sorry Harvey I was just thinking aloud." Linking her arm in his she walked with him towards the front entrance.

The imposing front door opened immediately the car stopped. Harvey was greeted by the butler with;"Good evening Sir, your mother is in the Parlour with the ladies and the Gentlemen are in the Library."

Turning towards Kate he went to take her coat, then seemed to hesitate only for a fraction of time but Kate picked up on it. Did she have a speck on her nose? It would have to wait until she was shown to her room.

A maid appeared at her elbow; "If you will come this way miss, I will show you to your room. Dinner is at eight-thirty, Madam kept it back until Mr Harvey arrived."

Opening the bedroom door the maid said, "I'm sure you will find everything you need but if you require anything else just ring the bell and someone will come at once."

Looking around Kate was impressed, a real fire in the hearth casting shadows on the walls, soft lighting, and a bathroom fit for a princess.

Unpacking her bag Kate was truly thankful she had packed a couple of dresses suitable for what was going to be a formal dinner. She was just about to fasten her second earring in place when there was a soft knock on her door. "Come in." she called, thinking it must be Harvey coming to fetch her to take her downstairs and introduce her to his family. But instead a very stately old lady entered, who immediately reminded Kate of her Great Aunt Grace.

Holding out her hand she introduced herself. "Hello I am Bethany, the senior Mrs Rutherford-Harris. My son's wife is the junior Mrs Rutherford -Harris. Kate who was rarely at a loss for words smiled, then taking the outstretched hand saying, "how do you do, I am Katherine McKenzie, usually called Kate, eldest daughter of my mother Elizabeth McKenzie Gibson and my late father Dr Skye McKenzie."

"Your mother has recently remarried I believe? She is very fortunate to have found a second husband at her age."

Before Kate could find a suitable reply without being rude, the indomitable old lady continued. "I myself could never countenance giving myself to another after promising to *love honour and obey.*"

This time Kate was ready, but what she was later to describe to her family as divine intervention, the dinner gong resounded through the house, ("did I say house more like a mansion.")

Smiling **sweetly** at the old lady Kate gestured towards the door. "Shall we go down?" Holding open the said door the senior Mrs Rutherford -Harris sailed through it calling over her shoulder. "Do close the door behind you my dear, it's what we do." placing the emphasis on the *-we*.

Harvey met them at the foot of the stairs.

"Darling I was just about to come and get you but I was waylaid. I see you have met Grandmother, I'm sure she will have kept you entertained."

Kate chose to ignore Harvey's remarks instead plastering a smile on her face, took his proffered arm and allowed him to take her into the dining room.

At first the room seemed to be overflowing with people, but within a few minutes all the guests were seated. There hadn't been time for any introductions but Harvey whispered to Kate, "after desert, coffee will be served in one of the formal reception rooms I will then introduce you to my immediate family. Usually eve of Thanksgiving is not as crowded as this but my parents had decided this year they would host a party for our Republican candidate. Tomorrow it will be family only. Of course that includes you darling."

The meal dragged on for hours or at least it seemed hours to Kate, at last her hostess rose from the table.

"Ladies - shall we leave the gentlemen to their port and cigars? Thirty minutes gentlemen," announced the junior Mrs Rutherford-Harris.

As Kate followed behind the female contingent, someone pulled the dining room door too closing out the collective sound of female voices.

A young woman leant over and whispered in Kate's ear, "I have to pinch myself this isn't a film set, it's almost pure *Gone with the Wind;* Kate grinned back "Except for the crinolines."

"Ah yes but only because the senior Mrs Rutherford-Harris hadn't thought of them," was the wicked reply "I'm Carol-Ann Browne with an *e,* what*'s* your name? Harvey didn't introduce us."

"Katherine Elizabeth McKenzie my family call me Kate."

"McKenzie; but surely that's Scottish."

"Yes you could say that but it's also a very familiar name in North America, New Zealand and in some parts of Africa, not forgetting Australia and Argentina. It all began with the Highland clearances way back a long time ago. An honourable name don't you think? And of course I'm certain there are just as many women named Katherine and Elizabeth as there are McKenzie's. Shall we go in Miss Carol-Ann Browne with an *e?*"

Harvey's mother was waiting for Kate inside the door. Taking Kate's hand said; "My dear I am so pleased to meet you, Harvey has told me so much about you. Now let me introduce you to some of the others; first the immediate family members." Kate smiled, shook innumerable hands doing what she was best at closing out her other senses. Suddenly she was aware someone was beside her, it was Carol-Ann.

"Kate may I call you Kate? You look as though you need something a tad stronger than coffee."

Turning to the younger woman at her side replied. "Thank you, but I rarely touch alcohol coffee will do, but I do have a rather troublesome headache. If you will excuse me I will return to my room, I carry emergency medication with me, usually if taken in time I avert a major migraine."

"Oh you poor thing, my elder sister suffers from those wretched headaches, would you like me to come with you?"

Placing her hand lightly on the younger woman's arm Kate assured her she would be fine once she had taken her tablets.

"Will you please make my apologies to Harvey's mother I will be down again presently."

Taking advantage of the ladies absence, the gentlemen sat down with their cigars and a drink of their choice. The absence of the ladies gave them the opportunity to talk about the forthcoming campaign to raise funds for the next Republican Candidate. Several of the older men were more conservative in their opinions and wanted more or less the same as before. While a few of the younger group wanted change, a radical approach to the twenty-first century.

Then cutting across the various arguments relative to this matter, Harvey's grandfather Rutherford-Harris changed the subject entirely.

"Harvey my boy, your Miss McKenzie, just how far down the road has your relationship gone?" Holding up his hand continued, "Let me finish then you can have your say."

"Grandfather this is not the time or the place to discuss such personal family matters." protested his grandson.

"Son these are family and very close friends and most are thinking along the same lines as me. You will be the fifth generation Rutherford -Harris to become the President of the Company and we are one of the oldest families hereabouts. We can trace our lineage back to the first settlers from the time of the Mayflower, and all I want to say is, remember that before you make any promises."

Unfortunately Kate was about to pass the dinning-room door when she heard what his grandfather said. She waited for Harvey to tell the bigoted old man to go to the Devil. Not a word, she heard a snigger then Grandfather laughed, and his companion repeated what he had whispered.

"Is she any good in the sack Harvey? I was told years ago some of the then half-breeds were real go-getters, if you get my meaning."

The silence was deafening, no-one spoke, and those who were in a position to see the door saw the figure of one Dr Katherine McKenzie slowly enter the room.

Kate directed her gaze towards Harvey, who sat as though turned to stone in an embarrassing silence. Speaking in a quiet voice as though she was talking to one of her sister's mother and baby group, addressed her remarks directly to Mr Rutherford – Harris senior.

"I will not sully the name gentleman by addressing you as such, because I doubt I should find one among you. I was invited to spend Thanksgiving with your grandson's family. It is therefore with regret I find I am unable to accept your hospitality after all. Harvey if you will arrange a flight for me to New York or failing that, a hire car with chauffeur to pick me up within the next sixty minutes. In the meantime finish your drinks- I'm sure the ladies will be expecting you to join them any minute now."

"Hold on there, Kate, Grandfather didn't mean to sound so rude it's just he is an old man and we must make allowances." As he said this he placed his hand on Kate's arm.

She gently removed Harvey's hand from her sleeve, don't push me Harvey because at this moment there is nothing I would like better than to spoil you very expensive teeth, now get the hell out of my way."

"Where are you going Kate?"

"I am are going home, back to Pipers Gate, it's where I belong just as you belong here with all the folks you know and love.

Tell your mother I had an urgent call home, or if you are man enough tell her the truth. You're good man Harvey forget the family firm for a while. Go back to Bosnia where you were doing so much good, better than being at the beck and call of your grandparents." Turning on her heal she left the room to return upstairs to repack her case. She was surprised to find she was not upset, annoyed yes, hopping mad at the old man's audacity yes, but most of all disappointed in Harvey. Here was a grown, educated man unable to face down a member of his family who had so crassly insulted a guest in the family home. She doubted if she would meet any of the Rutherford-Harris' family again anytime soon.

The butler came to her room and told her he had managed to get her a "hire car with   chauffeur," which would have her back in New York around five am.

Harvey was the only person to see her off.

"Kate will you allow me come to Pipers Gate sometime when this has blown over?"

Shaking her head replied, "I think not Harvey, what will be the point, we were good friends but nothing more than that. I think you should be brave and tell your family the truth."

Reaching up she kissed him one last time good bye, then stepped into the waiting car and was gone.

CHAPTER 2

"What What did Kate say exactly? I mean did she say what time she is due to arive?, I mean did she say what time she is due to arrive and where is she going to stay, here at Church House? Oliver put that down please. Daddy does not want a Tonker Truck on his tummy when he is holding Freddie."

Going to her son she gently removed the offending truck while at the same time giving him something more suitable to play with.

"All she said was I will be at Heath Row eight thirty pm, on the evening of the 18th. I didn't think to ask where she was staying but no doubt in the fullness of time we shall find out. After she called I telephoned your mother, she is all excited and yes she also asked the same question where is Kate going to stay? In the meantime Mrs Brice is making sure all is in order for Dr Kate's stay."

Reaching over the head of the second addition to the Page household Aubrey ran his lips over those of his wife. "I hope she intends to stay a while longer this time, perhaps even Christmas," Aubrey smiled at the thought. All the McKenzie's together under one roof, hopefully his and his Josephine's.

Putting his free hand behind his wife's neck Aubrey drew her head down for a second kiss, but with a teasing laugh she backed away. "Later sweetheart after our little people are fed and watered then tucked up in bed, we will play catch-up."

When Aubrey Page QC and Dr Josephine McKenzie had married and set up home in Church House, they had been in need of a resident Housekeeper and Gardener/ General Handyman. As luck would have it, Gordon Brice, Gardener to Josephine's mother at Pipers Gate, had a brother George, who was in need of a job. He had recently been made redundant by the Parks and Gardens division in Bury St Edmunds. He had two boys still at school and his wife worked as a part time career.

It was arranged this branch would meet with Mr Aubrey and Dr Josephine Page. Explaining it would be full time work, with generous time off but would mean they had to live in. At first Mrs Brice was more than a little dubious but when Aubrey explained they would have their own house, or rather all the rooms over the building which had been the stables for their own personal use. Of course these would have to be brought up to date then they could move in once the conversion work was completed.

Now almost three and a half years later the house ran like clockwork, and not for the first time when Josephine had returned home from afternoon surgery, one or both the Brice boys were sprawled on the floor of the room the family used as their own private parlour, playing with Oliver, the first born Page, his daddy's pride and joy. With the advent of a second son Freddie some seventeen months ago, the youngest Brice boy was content to sit with the either Oliver or Freddie, or more often than not both little boys telling them about his day at school.

Aubrey found the boys interest in his infant children fascinating, he learned what they had been up to during their school day, what they thought about their teachers and, most of all the love and affection they showed towards their parents. George Brice, their father didn't believe in smacking, he reckoned it didn't solve anything except breed resentment between parent and child. By the same token his boys had to toe the line and learn that unacceptable behaviour had consequences. Aubrey was intrigued by what he termed the *Brice method*, nurture, love and acceptable discipline in equal measure from both parents.

When Aubrey remarked upon this to his wife she had reminded him all families were not like the Brice family. Josephine could remember only too well the Watson-Hopes. It was amazing they were quite content to leave their little daughter Amanda in residential care for so long.

Later when they had put the children to bed, and were settled down, the main topic of conversation was Kate, Josephine's twin.

"While you were attending to Freddie, Sebastian phoned wanting news of Kate's ETA but I couldn't tell him any more than what we already know."

"It's OK love," responded Josephine, "Patrick phoned her earlier and managed to catch her before she left for the airport. From the little Kate said it looks as though she is maybe coming home for a fairly long stay."

"All we can do is to possess our souls in patience until sometime tomorrow. Now come here woman and give your long suffering husband a cuddle." Suiting actions to words Aubrey swooped down upon his wife, scooped her up and sat down again with her firmly on his lap.

"Now then love of my life, have you written out your Christmas list, no not the things we have to do before the great day, but what you would like in your stocking from your besotted husband."

"Ah; now let me think, what do you say to a holiday with palm trees, silver sand, and you, just to myself for two whole weeks?." Smiling into the face of the man who held her, Josephine noticed he had a few more silver threads among his still dark hair. How she loved this man, material possessions meant nothing to her, without Aubrey Page her life would have no meaning, with him she had everything, he was her lover, husband and very best friend.

"Speaking of Sebastian, is he and his little brood coming to stay here or going to Pipers Gate for Christmas? It would be nice if they came here the boys will be three, we could have a birthday party for them; it would be fun."

"Aubrey my love you are quite a glutton for punishment. Enough about Santa Claus, have you forgotten we are all invited to spend Christmas at Pipers Gate and then everybody is returning here on or about the 28/29th December so we can celebrate New Year at Church House. This time the children are a little older and with Miriam in charge, we can have a grown up celebration to welcome in the New Year."

"Providing we don't have any road accidents or expected babies arriving early."

Josephine bent and kissed her smiling husband."Don't tempt providence love I still haven't forgotten that dreadful accident the night of Patricks wedding and then Sebastian in a panic just before Christmas three years ago when Christina went into premature labour."

Aubrey remembered all too clearly the night of 14th February 1995. His beloved Josephine had been called to out to the scene of a truly dreadful road accident to assist with the injured and dying. He recalled the sickening fear when she didn't come home for hours, the despair at the thought of losing her, and sheer relief when she finally returned home. Yes he could understand Sebastian initial panic, and yet he had quickly brought him emotions under control and delivered the first of his boys while waiting for the ambulance as though he had delivered scores of babies in the rear of his car. Sebastian admitted to his brother-in-law later he had never been so scared in his life.

"Changing the subject darling, is Daniel going to host a Horky next March?"

"I'm not sure, to date he hasn't mentioned it but that doesn't mean he isn't. Has he mentioned anything to you?"

Aubrey took his time in answering his wife's question, at this particular time he didn't want to commit himself before he and his stepfather-in-law had an opportunity to discuss what was at this stage, just a germ of an idea.

Professor Daniel Gibson, the McKenzie Step -Papa was a great hand in arranging surprise parties. He had arranged a fabulous party for his wedding reception; this had been recorded in the Parish of Brackonfield, as the best party the village had known over the last fifty years or so. He had also gone on to do a repeat performance for his first, second and third wedding anniversaries, so this next one may well be different. Aubrey kept his own counsel. Daniel on his last visit to Church House had been sounding Aubrey out about doing a full scale

Gilbert and Sullivan performance with a family party to finish up the evening. It all depended on the completion of the work being carried out on the remaining part of the stable block. This was scheduled to become a state of the art music centre, with a stage and floor space for dancing holding parties, and above all, making music. It was being sound proofed to the highest specifications so not to disturb the Brice family. Although it was more than likely the boys would be included in some of the musical offerings, as the eldest, Derek was learning to play the guitar, while the youngest William known as Wills, was still playing the recorder but hoped to be promoted to the drums. (Not any time soon was his father's earnest prayer).

Just then a fretful wail was heard on the baby alarm. "I'll go love you have had him all day. Poor little boy, his mouth is quite painful cutting his back molars is making him restless. Hopefully they will be through in the next couple of days. Will you check on Oliver, see you upstairs." Planting a kiss on Aubrey's forehead Josephine took herself off to attend their youngest child.

Looking down at the child in her arms, Josephine felt such a wealth of love wash over her. She never went to sleep without thanking whoever was out there looking out for her and her loved ones. She and Aubrey had created and made two beautiful children, and in the fullness of time would make at least two more.

It was time her twin sister settled down and started a family, but first she had to make up her mind about one Professor Charles Blossom.

CHAPTER 3

FRIDAY 18TH DECEMBER 1998

The departure lounge was heaving. Several departures were delayed for a variety of reasons, the main one snow, and by the sound of the tannoy system lots of it. In the majority of cases the snow was sweeping down from Canada thus causing problems for USA domestic flights to the north and west of New York.

Kate had been waiting the statutory three hours for her flight to Heath Row London, and was praying her's would be one of the few which left on time.

Her prayers were about to be answered, the tannoy once again blared forth. ."Will all passengers for the 10.50 hours flight to Heath Row London please go to gate 6 immediately, this plane will take off immediately the passengers are on board."

It was the last little piece of information which had Kate wondering why the sudden hurry, not that she was complaining; she wanted to go home as soon as possible.

As she waited her turn to board she went back over in her mind the last three very hectic weeks.

After her sudden departure from the Rutherford-Harris gathering she had immediately started to pack her belongings ready for shipping back to the U.K. Plus to make arrangements to wind up the lease on her apartment, and what she couldn't take with her she gave to various friends. Fortunately Kate had undertaken to take only the first semester of the college year, thus leaving UCL NY would not cause any disruption to her students.

However on what was to be her last day the Dean of the Faculty had asked if she would reconsider and stay for the 2nd semester beginning in January, but Kate had graciously declined his offer?

."I have enjoyed working with the students very much and their interaction and hard work was very gratifying, but I have stayed away from my native shores for far too long."

So it was on that last day as a lecturer and in some cases mentor, Kate bade her students fair-well. She had hoped she would just slip away, but students past and present decided she was to have a going away party. Just after close of play for the day the Dean sent for her, he wanted to have a few words before she left.

Kate knocked on the office door, a voice called enter, she opened the door and it seemed as all hell let loose, but no, just the place was crowded with bodies all calling"Surprise Surprise."

"You didn't really believe we would let you go as easy as that," called one of her students "The best lecturer in the business." called another. ."Order Order!." someone bellowed.

There was instant hush. ."Dr McKenzie, Kate it has been our great pleasure to have you with us this past five years. You have taught us many things outside our immediate circle, to look at the bigger picture. Not to be afraid to take from other cultures ideas out of our own comfort zone. To go out to meet new challenges in the world of environmental engineering, not to destroy but to build; to take up old ideas and graft on the new. To understand what it all means, in order to make a big difference for future generations.   I'm sure you are all familiar with Dr McKenzie's Pilgrims Prayer - but for the benefit of those of you who have forgotten let me quote it to you.

A Pilgrim's Prayer.

To do the best you can, Help those you can,
Have the courage to what is right even in the face of adversity,
And when you fail, have the courage to pick yourself up

and try again.
Because in the end we do not own this land we live on,
But are the custodians for the next generation.
Let the Stars in the heavens by your guide
There you will find your God."

Taking Kate's hand in his the Dean bent and kissed her on each cheek saying,

"Thank you Dr Katherine McKenzie you brought a breath of fresh air into our academic minds, God Speed." This was greeted by thunderous applause.

She waited until it was once again quiet then someone called Speech! Speech!

Turning towards her fellow academics then to the students before her Kate stood tall, her back straight, and more than a little humbled.

"Today I'm leaving to return to the UK but for so long as I live I will never forget your kindness, your work and achievements. When I first came here I wondered what I had let myself in for. Previously I have done lecture tours, research work and lots of diverse studies in other cultural work places etc. But one of my greatest pleasures was meeting new young minds ready to embrace the world of knowledge, some for the exploration of other ethnic peoples. Some of you to expand the knowledge of your own immediate surroundings on how to change things for the better; and a small, but very vital minority, to explore knowledge for its own sake. Students past and present of UCL NY I salute you." Raising her hands above her head she clapped, soon the room echoed with applause for her.

It had been an experience she would not ever forget.

A Hand on her arm jerked her back to the present. "It is your turn Miss, would you like some help? Is it the first time for you?" Kate looked blank. "Your first flight, I know it can be a bit nerve racking at first but once we take off you will be fine."

Kate smiled at the woman who was trying to reassure her.

"I'm fine I was miles away plus a very late night, I will have a snooze once we are under way. But thank you for your concern."

The elderly lady just nodded but she knew it was more than that, she recognised the look of sheer raw unhappiness. She herself had trodden that particular path in her younger days.

The flight was uneventful and arrived bang on time, however, before disembarking the passengers had been advised the temperature outside was -2.Celsius It was cold with a capital C.

It was Kate's intention to go straight to Bedford Square and stay with Patrick and his Lucy for a couple of nights before continuing to Pipers Gate in time for Christmas.

Patrick and Lucy, together with Elizabeth and Daniel were all waiting as she came out of customs into the arrivals hall.

At the sight of her family all frantically waving to attract her attention, Kate felt her eyes tear up.

"I will not cry I will not cry." she muttered to herself but obviously she wasn't listening because the first thing she did was hold on to Daniel of all people and cry like a child. Holding her close as though she was once again a little girl Daniel cuddled her to him at the same time trying to take his handkerchief out of his pocket.

Patrick seeing his Step-Papa's predicament handed him his with a grin. Then a well remembered voice cut in-

"Are you all going to stand here all night? If we have to hang around much longer we will be stuck to the ground, its bloody freezing out here. Kate you will have to continue your crying jag when we get home."

"Christopher, Oh I've missed you, all of you so much, and I'm starving."

Her tears drying up miraculously Kate was led towards the car park.

"I'm so pleased to see you all, I was only expecting Patrick and perhaps Lucy but all the rest of you."

"We persuaded Sebastian to stay home, he's coming to Pipers Gate early on Christmas Eve with his family, just in time for their little boys third birthday.

Josephine and Aubrey with their two boys are also coming Christmas Eve in time for the birthday party. We will already be there, me and Daniel, Patrick and Lucy, Lucy's half brother and sister, which just leaves you Christopher."

"Yes Ma I know but first I have a meeting tomorrow with John and Sybil Buchanan then I will come to Pipers Gate on either 23rd or 24th December, then all being well will be going to Church House on the 30th December until 2nd January. I promised Josephine and Aubrey to see the New Year in with them.

So little sister you are going to be here for your twin nephews third birthday and to renew your acquaintance with your other two small nephews?"

"My goodness this is posh, who does this very modern machine belong to?" Kate was standing beside a shiny black seven seater four wheel drive.

"Ours." Just one word but filled with pride. "Being grandparents brings special responsibilities, our other car does not have the capacity for child car seats and all the paraphernalia modern children need when travelling from one home to another. Besides I get quite a kick out of driving it around, especially with all the children on board," Daniel grinned at his wife. "So does grandma here. Come on now young Kate let's be having you, straight home Patrick and don't spare the horses."

CHAPTER 4

Jim Harris must have been watching out for the car because as soon as it stopped outside number 27 Bedford Square he swung open the front door and ushered them into the vestibule greeting each member of the family by name.

"It is lovely to have you back with us Dr Kate, everything is in place Professor as you ordered, Mum has laid on a hot buffet, so go on up I will see to your luggage." Suiting actions to words Jim Harris Butler/Bodyguard/Right hand man to McKenzie S.I Ltd began to unload Kate's cases.

"So you haven't missed having Heather around, I must say your friend Mr Harris seems to have become almost indispensable." commented Kate with a sly grin, "and I take it he has a Mrs Harris who acts as housekeeper for you."

"Not quite, it's not a wife she is his mother. She lives in Heather's old quarters and Jim is at present in the basement. Christopher's old rooms." replied Lucy pausing outside the door to what had been Elizabeth's domain. "You might find some of the changes we, that is Patrick and me have made to what was your mother's domain a little different but in keeping with the house. Welcome home Kate." Opening the door she ushered them all into what had been Elizabeth's drawing room. At first it looked more or less the same as before, but taking a second good hard look Kate could several small but subtle changes to the décor and soft furnishings.

Kate turned to her mother to see if she showed any emotion at the changes, then said "Lucy it looks gorgeous, it looks almost the same and yet it's not. I love it."

Lucy had been holding her breath, and as her husband took her hand in his whispered, "Its O.K love I told you she would understand."

"Understand what." asked his sister?

"We thought you might resent us making changes to what was your home."

"Patrick come here and let me hug you, this is now yours and Lucy's home, you live here all the year round so of course you will want to have your own things round you and from what I have noticed in the short time I have been here it's been so tastefully done it still looks like home.

"Is anybody going to start eating, I'm starving I haven't eaten since lunch time it's about time I did," moaned Christopher.

"Oh for the love of heaven come on then" with that throw away remark Kate followed her brother into the dining-room where a hot buffet was laid out with food keeping hot on top of an assortment of hot plates.

"So tell me again who is going to Pipers Gate and when?"

"Kate, don't talk with your mouth full you are bad as your brother, pass me one of those things which look like hot pancakes please."

Elizabeth's two youngest children looked on in amazement. "She never changes does she," Christopher grinning pointed towards his mother. "I think our Ma doesn't know we are now fully paid up members of the grownups world." Their mother wisely chose to make no comment.

So tell me who is going to Pipers Gate and when." Kate fixed her stare on her middle brother, "Patrick?"

Holding up his hand ticked his fingers in turn.

"Ma with our Step Papa later tomorrow, Lucy and I on the 23rd. Sebastian and his family plus Aubrey and his Josephine with their little brood just before tea time on the 24th so you can take your pick which day you choose to travel. However for convenience sake perhaps you will come with Lucy and me."

"Fiona and Michael are already there. I collected Fiona from college earlier this week and Michael travelled down from Edinburgh yesterday. You do of course know that although McKenzie S.I was made responsible for them in a supervisory capacity.

Your mother and I have been appointed their legal guardians until they are twenty-one," Daniel commented quietly.

"Daniel has a great capacity for giving, this can encompass loving guidance as well as gentle discipline and plus, in fact a very big plus, we make these young people know they are part of our family. Something which was taken away from them due to circumstances they did not understand," this was said with a quiet pride by Elizabeth. Looking towards her partner with a love all too evident to see she turned back to her daughter.

"Kate if you will excuse us we are off to our bed. We will see you in the morning before going to Suffolk, sleep well." Giving Kate a kiss and one last hug she and Daniel left, leaving the three siblings together with Lucy.

It wasn't long before Lucy showed Kate her room. "We didn't make any changes here apart from the basic maintenance, the curtains are new but I tried to get more or less the same as before."

Kate looked round what had been her room for more years than she cared to remember. She felt her eyes tear up yet again. Everybody was so kind to her and she felt she didn't deserve it. Staying away from her family for so many years just to keep out of Jamie Tallington's way; running away more like it and for what' ?Asked that still small voice inside her head. Well it was time to stop running she had lost so much time when she could have had a husband and children of her own by now. Saying nothing of her thoughts to her sister-in-law, Kate smiled and assured Lucy she was so pleased to be home nothing else mattered.

CHAPTER 5

Josephine put the phone down gently, although she had expected her twin to telephone her after she had rested she didn't expect to wait until the day before Christmas Eve to hear from her. Then when she had and they had exchanged the usual hellos and how are you? The first thing she had asked was she hoped no one invited any of the Tallington tribe to Pipers Gate over the holidays.

"Trouble love, I take it that was your sister, you seem upset."

Looking over her shoulder she smiled at her husband, no not upset, more perplexed she still has this hang up over Jamie Tallington, and the sad part is I thought she had put whatever it was with our Mr J Tallington to bed after Sebastian's wedding."

"It appears we were wrong, but something went on there, because not long after, one Professor Charles Fitzroy Blossom disappears from the scene for a while."

"He came to our wedding with Kate but he seemed a little withdrawn. As though he came because he had already accepted our invitation then once the garden project was completed he goes off to China on a rare plant expedition."

"Has he returned yet?"

"I'm not aware if he has actually returned. I do know he writes to young Con Rogers on a regular basis."

Aubrey took his time in replying, "Josephine do you think Jamie Tallington had a word with our young Professor at either of our weddings, Sebastian's or ours?"

"What kind of word are you thinking about?" Josephine inquired.

"The kind something such as; Keep of the grass friend she is my girl friend and we had a tiff but once we can have a conversation in private I'm sure we will sort ourselves out again etc."

"That could possibly be the cause Charles backed off, leaving the field clear for Jamie Tallington." pondered Josephine, "but surely Kate must have told Charles she hadn't spoken to Tallington for almost twelve years or more?"

"Not necessarily so, just remember when they met, Charles Blossom appeared to have fallen for your sister hook, line and sinker, and by the look on Kate's face at the time, so had she. The sad thing was neither of them appeared to know. I remember when I was with your three brothers when we were discussing who would take on the Shawcross youngsters, we all thought the next McKenzie wedding would be Kate and Charles Blossom."

"Well my love there is nothing we can do until we get to Pipers Gate and in the meantime we have a small job to do, called packing presents ready for transportation to Grandma and Grandpa's house."

"Have we time for a cuddle before we start the day?" Aubrey asked with a hopeful smile.

"I'll always have time for you love, but for now, just the one." Josephine relied with a laugh.

Sometime later Josephine emerged from the bathroom to the sound of squeals of laughter coming from further along the corridor. Aubrey was on his hands and knees playing at growly bear with Oliver. The little boy of two years and six months was having a high old time of it pretending to be frightened, while his daddy was obviously enjoying playing with his son.

"Where is Freddie?" addressing her question to her beloved, Josephine waited for him to reply, but it was Oliver who spoke.

"Mimi took him, Freddie cried, he's hungry. Daddy Bear hungry, me is hungry, Mummy hungry? Crouching down so she was eye to eye with both of them asked,

"Who would like hot pancakes with Maple syrup for breakfast?" Giving the two of them a swift kiss on the mouth she hurried down to the kitchen to check on her youngest boy, all of seventeen months.

She found him sitting in his high-chair with Miriam feeding him his breakfast.

"Good morning Miriam your must have got here early, it's just barely gone eight o'clock

"Its fine Dr Jo I was up early so I thought I would come along and help with the boys; I know you have an early surgery today, so here I am."

Josephine never ceased to bless the day when Miriam Khan had entered the lives of the Aubrey- Page family. She had been expecting Oliver and was having a pretty hectic time; what with supervising the furnishing of Church House, working in the specialised medical practise in Cambridge, and commuting from Pipers Gate every day throughout the week. Fortunately she had been spared the dreaded morning sickness and Aubrey took his impending fatherhood very seriously, insisting his wife rested whenever possible. His attention to detail was as consistent as it had been when he was a high court judge. This had caused hilarity amongst the McKenzie family when their first born arrived at precisely three o 'clock on the afternoon 27th May 1996. Bang on time for Josephine and Aubrey's first wedding anniversary. The time was an added bonus, the exact time they had exchanged their wedding vows.

However, let us to return to the arrival of one Miss Miriam Khan. She had appeared in the village during late autumn several months prior to Oliver's birth, carrying a back-pack and nothing more. Miriam had stopped off at the vicarage to ask for directions to Foxton. Explaining she was trying to trace the Roman way across the Chilterns. Soon she and the vicar, then one or two of the locals joined in the debate which was the best way to go, when Aubrey came upon them. It was at that point Miriam seemed to draw herself in.

"Thank you all for your help but I must go now." But before she could leave Aubrey placed a gentle hand on her arm.

"You don't have to leave because of me. I'm pleased to see you looking so well."

Miriam stood still her first instinct had been to run, but she done nothing wrong why should she run away from the man who had been responsible for putting that dreadful man who called himself her father, away for almost the rest of his natural life.

"Miriam look at me, how are you coping? It must be nearly five years since we last met."

"I'm O.K I suppose, I still have nightmare occasionally but at least I can please myself where I go and what I do."

"Are you working?"

"No not yet, nobody wants someone like me."

"What did you do when you left school?

"Worked for a time in our local nursery, I wanted to train as a nursery nurse or a proper nanny. There is a very good training school in North London, where you are trained properly in all aspects of child care from new born to preschoolers.

Of course after the trial it was out of the question, nobody would want me, you know old saying."No smoke without fire."

Aubrey Page lately a High Court Judge could think on his feet and in this instance his brain went into what he was to call later, overdrive.

"Miriam, if I can get you into this Posh Training school for Top Notch Nannies will you join us to live and work in Church House as a Nanny when you finish the course? We have a baby due in about five months or so, and my wife, who is a doctor, will need a Top Notch Nanny when our babe is about six months old or maybe before then."

Miriam didn't say anything she just stood there silent and looking at the man before her, burst into tears. One of the women who had been talking to Miriam stepped forward, and put an arm round the weeping woman's shoulders.

"What did you say to her to make her cry like this, you should be ashamed of yourself Mr Page making this poor girl all upset."

"Shaking her head Miriam gave a hiccough saying."No he hasn't upset me; he has just saved my life."

"Well he has a funny way of showing it, if you ask me," she replied with a slight sniff.

Holding out his hand Aubrey suggested Miriam accompanied him home to meet Josephine. "Everybody round here call her Dr Jo, let's go round to Church House, we will find her there; she is supervising the people who are hanging the curtains."

So it had come to pass Miriam did her nursery training, and finished in time to join the Aubrey-Page household when Oliver was almost nine months old. Then Freddie arrived so Miriam had two babies to care for. Oliver fifteen months old and Freddie brand new. She was to explain later to one Christopher McKenzie it was the beginning to the happiest time in her life.

CHAPTER 6

Kate chose to travel back to the family home with Patrick and Lucy. During the drive Lucy was bringing her sister-in-law up to date with all that had been happening to the Patrick branch of McKenzie S.I.

"You remember all the Who-Ha there was about the new window for Daniel's Institute."

"You mean about the window itself or the fact Sebastian thought you had used Patrick as your model?"

"Actually both, when Sebastian first saw the drawings he said it was the image of Patrick, but when he scrutinised it properly he said it was more like their dead father."

"I had not deliberately used Patrick as a model I think in my subconscious mind I saw Patrick as a guide and protector, an epitome of all that is good."

"At first I was both amazed and flattered, then like Sebastian I was humbled, my lovely Lucy, despite all that had happened to her was able to draw something so beautiful, and using the McKenzie's as a model for her remarkable Angel Gabriel. We are all so very proud of her." this last statement was directed towards his wife with such loving pride it made Kate wish someone would look at her in such a way. No, not someone, Charles Blossom, unconsciously she rubbed her hand where her heart was supposed to be.

"Ma never mentioned it when she wrote."

"No to both your questions. After the drawing was accepted by the committee it was decided in view of how much it would cost to make, engrave, and install it would be better to commence the actual contractual work during 1998 and have the installation done by the end of 1999 then the grand unveiling on the 1st January 2000 the major work of the Millennium. I tried to keep the initial drawing a secret from Patrick. It was indirectly responsible for my voice coming back."

"How well you succeeded my love." Patrick gave his wife a sidelong glance which made Kate catch her breath. After nearly four years of marriage her brother was still head over heels in love with his Lucy.

"What time is Sebastian due to arrive? I can't wait to see the twins .The last time I saw them was when I came over to see Josephine when she had Freddie and he is very nearly seventeen month old." remarked Kate, she felt tired and out of sorts with herself. For the first time in a long while she pondered on the *'what if'* syndrome. Suppose she hadn't gone off to America, *'what if* she hadn't run from Jamie, *'what if'* but here she stopped. She had and she did. What was the use making a song and dance about whom, or what was to blame, it was she who chose to run, nobody made her physically do it.

Lucy thought she heard a sob from behind her, she listened intently; it was a sob quickly followed another.

Leaning towards her husband Lucy spoke softly so only he could hear said," about a mile away is a comfort stop where you can rest up and have a hot drink or whatever, I think it is about time we had a break."

Patrick did not have to be told twice, he too had heard the sobs from the back seat.

Driving into the car park Patrick said, "Ladies I think a thirty minutes break is in order, the loo is on the right and the café `is straight ahead. I will catch up with you both in the café`."

Once out of the car Kate made for the café she had hoped her brother and Lucy had not noticed her distress. As soon as she was inside Lucy took her arm and gently steered her towards a vacant table away from the crowd.

"Patrick will be with us in a moment before he comes would you care to tell me what is making you so upset?" Looking at the woman before her Lucy wanted to put her arms around the slight figure and gave her a hug. "The questions can keep until later when you are ready to talk but Kate I really think it should be sooner than later." Just at that moment Patrick arrived with a tray of coffees and assorted cakes.

"I didn't bring too much because if I know our Heather she will have killed the fatted calf," "plus half the local turkeys as well." finished of Kate with a tearful smile.

Kate didn't have time for further introspection; she was immediately surrounded by her family.

"I will take your bags upstairs Doctor McKenzie said the quiet voice of Mr Benson, Elizabeth and Daniel's very proper butler. It is good to have you home." Giving him a friendly smile Kate thanked him.

"Where's my precious girl then, it's so good to have you with us for Christmas." The voice was that of Heather Wilson. Finding herself cradled in Heather's arms almost had Kate in tears yet again.

Holding the woman away from her Heather said; "This is going to be a forever Christmas young lady, no more running away from us. Having you home makes this family complete. Now come along we are all getting ready for a very special occasion. We have two little boys who are to celebrate their third Birthday tomorrow, but first of all we have a welcome home celebration to hold especially for you."

Ushering a bewildered Kate before her, Heather opened the door to the small dining-room with a flourish. The table was set with what looked to be a mountain of food and right in the middle was one large iced cake inscribed *Welcome Home Long May You Stay*. And it had all the McKenzie names written in a variety of coloured icing. "We were going to keep it until tomorrow when Sebastian and Josephine's families arrive but your Ma said it wouldn't be the same especially when we are to have two little boys with their birthday cake."

"Heather its perfect, we will save some for the rest of the family when they arrive tomorrow. So Heather, Ma, Step Papa, Patrick and Lucy hang on just a minute." Going out into hall Kate caught up with Mr Benson. "Mr Benson will you come and have some of my stupendous, *welcome home cake*. Heather has really and truly surpassed herself this time." Returning to the dining-room Kate spoke to them all   "This is the very best homecoming ever. I never expected anything like this, I always thought," here she stopped

"Thought what love." asked her mother in a gentle voice.

"I don't really know, I wasn't very important, being away from home so much I sort of felt cut off, not part of you or what you did. Somehow I had this feeling what I did or who I was didn't matter any-more." Taking a deep breath Kate continued;"later, before all the family disperse after the Christmas holiday, for those of you who may be interested I will try to explain the initial reason why I left all those years ago so suddenly, and the reason why this year I have just as suddenly decided to stop running away. Now shall we eat?"

Elizabeth very wisely decided not to probe any further, well at least not until after the holiday was over then she and her elder twin daughter were going to have a heart to heart talk.

"Daniel, this year Christmas is going to be special, I cannot remember when the last time Kate was home. She always had an excuse of one kind or another."

Taking off his reading glasses Daniel put his book aside. "Has any of the Tallington family ever told you exactly what happened between Jamie and Kate all those years ago, because from what I know of our Kate it must have been something very bad? She is not the type to up and run then keep on running for all these past years. Then she introduced Mr Harvey Rutherford-Harris into the family circle. You know Elizabeth I couldn't quite figure that out. There was no love there, friendship yes but nothing else. You know what I think? She brought the Yank here hoping everybody would think he was her boyfriend / partner. Has she said where he is now?"

"My dear I'm as much in the dark as you, but he most certainly is not coming for Christmas, she would have said so by now, it's only two days away."

Standing together before the window in what was known as Grandpa's study Elizabeth and Daniel looked out at the winter afternoon sky turning from pink then to red, then dark indigo, heralding a sharp frost. Elizabeth gave a small sigh as her husband drew her head down onto his shoulder. "It is going to be a cold one tonight love, let's go and join the others." dropping a light kiss on her brow. "Tomorrow will see the rest of family arrive."

"With the exception of Christopher," murmured his mother.

"Yes Christopher is coming, I persuaded him to defer joining the Buchanan family until the New Year. I explained this could be the last opportunity to be with all the McKenzie family under one roof."

"What do you mean Daniel?"

"I may be wrong love, but Sebastian and Christina's family are growing up quickly and they may, as might Josephine and Aubrey, want to spend Christmas in their own homes, especially if any one decides to add to the McKenzie family tree."

"Daniel Gibson, do you know something that I don't?"

"Not at all sweetheart, but we have three ladies, who shall we say are not content to rest upon their laurels. Now come along wife it's time to join the family."

CHAPTER 7

Christmas Eve can be a stressful time for parents at the best of times but in one of the McKenzie families they had the extra excitement of two small people celebrating a third birthday."

"Have you packed Teddy Edward Daddy?" "And my Aussie Teddy." piped a second voice.

"Yes Cameron and yes Alistair your bears are both safe and sound in the back with your cases." Sebastian had been up since just after six am, he had packed most of the requisite cases plus Christmas gifts the night before, just leaving the last minute personal items to be added to the luggage. The special car seats for his sons were more or less always in situ so that was one less chore to think about.

"Boys come and have your faces washed then it will be time to leave."

"We was washed before breakfast."

"Were washed, not was washed" admonished their school teacher mother.

"Alistair you have milk all around your mouth and Cameron you had better clean your teeth."

"Why?"

"Because that is what we do after eating."

"Do you mean both of us or just me?"

"Both of you, now let's get a move on; we are going to have such a lovely day."

Glancing at her husband Christina grinned in his direction.

"Your sons are almost ready, if you will keep an eye on them while I finish checking we haven't forgotten anything then we can be off."

Sebastian nodded his agreement; the love of his life had handling the twins off to a fine art. It must be something to do with the fact Christina was a school teacher when they were married in April 1995, but they hadn't expected to produce twin boys on the 24th December that same year. They had moved into Pipers Gate with the babies until Sebastian could find a bigger house for his family. This took more time than he had anticipated, because the price of property in Richmond was rapidly rising out of all proportion to its worth.

However Aubrey Page came to the rescue. Aubrey became a silent partner in McKenzie S.I. Ltd and instead of putting actual cash into the business he invested in property which meant Sebastian was able to become a tenant of McKenzie S.I. Ltd

After a period of commuting from Pipers Gate to London they moved to a large Victorian house with a good size garden just a short distance away from Richmond Park.

Christina missed her little house in Mayfield Row but realised once the babies arrived it would be way too small.

"Right are we all aboard? Let's be off then." As Sebastian drove away he asked if anyone would like to sing.

"Yes came a chorus of voices." "Jingle bells Jingle bells," called out the little boys."

"OK that will do for a start then we will sing some carols."

"What's carols Mummy?"

"Special Christmas songs Alistair, listen Daddy and me will sing the first line then see if you can sing it."

"Me too, I can sing."

"Yes you too Cameron. Are you ready? Right here we go." Christina started to sing Away in a Manger, Sebastian joined in and soon the little boys after a few false starts were able to join in even if they didn't get the words quite right.

"Are we nearly there." the perpetual call of small children everywhere.

"Yes but before we arrive we are going to have a comfort stop."

"Why."

"Because I need to stretch my legs and you two need to visit the toilet."

"Daddy, will you come with us?"

"Yes Cameron me as well, we don't want to arrive at Grandma and Grandpa's house uncomfortable do we?"

Two pairs of dark eyes looked at their daddy. "Why."

Christina gave in to a gurgle of laughter.

"Because we think you should so come along the pair of you."

Once the necessary ablutions had been completed, the children strapped into the car seats, Sebastian resumed their journey. It wasn't very long before the car turned between the gates which gave the house its name.

As the house came into view the children bounced with excitement.

"We're here." Christina gave a sigh of pure joy.

"Just look at the trees outside the front door, Daniel must have done this." Sebastian leaned over and buzzed his lips against his wife's mouth. "In all the excitement don't forget how much I love you."

Placing her hand on his thigh she squeezed it gently before kissing him back.

"I'll never forget love, ever." Then with a wicked smile said, "You are all mine."

The front door opened."Welcome, all of you and how are my Boyos?" Daniel looked larger than life wearing a red Santa Claus hat trimmed with fake white fur. Opening his arms wide Daniel gathered two excited little boys to him.

"Come along in we have lots for you two to do before tea-time, so let's be having you."

Christina and Sebastian followed the exuberant Host into the hall.

"This year someone has gone OTT." remarked a grinning Sebastian. The hall had been turned into a fairyland. White and silver garlands adorned the ceiling and looped down the stair- way walls. A Christmas tree over twelve feet high stood in the stairwell rising majestically up past the first floor banisters. Round the walls were garlands of green fir, holly and of course mistletoe.

"Wow, my goodness someone has been busy." Daniel tried to look suitably modest but failed he just couldn't keep his face straight.

"It was a joint effort, Gordon and his brother George did all the clambering about but me and your Ma designed it. But come on inside there is still work to be done and these two young men will be needed to help until we have reinforcements later on."

"What is forcement Grandpa?" Cameron held on to Daniel's hand.

"Will we like what Cameron said Grandpa?" Alistair asked. Hunkering down before the two little boys Daniel put an arm round each child.

"The word is re-in-force-ments- there I have broken it up into small pieces, I bet you can't say it."

"Yes we can, we can do anything hard if we stick together, that why we are called twins." Two pairs of earnest eyes gazed directly back at their Grandpa Daniel."

"The word means until some more help comes."

"What help?" this time it was asked by Alistair.

Daniel was rescued by their Grandma Beth (when very young they couldn't get their tongues around Elizabeth)

"Come with me and see." Ushering them into the main drawing room she showed them another Christmas tree but not quite as big. But there was a difference, this tree had one or two baubles on it but no tinsel and although the fairy lights were already strung through the branches, they were not turned on.

"When everybody has arrived and we have all had our tea, we will dress the tree. But first of all we have two birthdays to celebrate. Can anyone guess who?"

"It's us! It's us!" cried two excited children. "We are going to be three, see we have our birthday badges on, they have the number three on them."

In the midst of the general hubbub Josephine and Aubrey arrived with their two sons. Oliver aged two years and six months and, Freddie a toddler, of just short of seventeen months.

Spying their Aunty and Uncle, Cameron and Alistair dashed over to them and each child grabbing a leg of their uncle Aubrey.

"Its Unca Aub." they chorused," we are now three, see look at our badges we got them before we come here."

Aubrey passed his youngest son to Josephine, then bending down picked each child clinging to his legs and swinging them in tandem one under each arm cried. "Grandpa shall I put them on the top of the Christmas tree?" Both children shrieked in pretend fear.

"Put them down Uncle Aubrey you'll make them sick." broke in Josephine "besides they don't much look like fairies to me."

"Not Fairies we are Boys." they laughed in unison.

By the time the birthday cake had been cut and partially eaten, both sets of parents were more than ready for a quiet sit down.

Patting the seat next to her Josephine invited her sister to take the weight of her legs. As an aunt of four boisterous nephews Kate had joined in the birthday games with gusto.

Kate sank into her seat, "goodness they take some energy, Christina how do you cope and do part time teaching too?"

"Kate the trick is called delegation, I am extremely lucky. You remember Shona Douglas the young lady who was Lucy's only attendant at her wedding, well, her mother is a widow with two younger children, twins a boy and a girl who are now almost twelve. When we moved house Sebastian had an idea, he suggested we invited Mrs Douglas to work for us as general factotum, much the same as Heather did or rather does for Ma. Anyway she said yes so she comes five days a week and Pansy, her youngest daughter dotes on the boys. Plus quite a number of the senior students at St Paul's are queuing up to baby-sit. Now Kate tell us all about exciting things which have been happening to you in the 'Big Apple' and just as a matter of interest who did you bring home with you this time?"

"Sorry ladies I came home with just me." Then swiftly changing the subject asked had anything been heard about the fate of Lucy's step father.

Before Kate could continue she felt a hand gently squeeze her shoulder while a dark head leant down towards hers.

"Not now Kate, this is a time of rejoicing we will play catch up later, that is if you intend to stay with us long enough."

"Patrick, I'm sorry of course I don't want to upset Lucy I just wondered."

"Wondered what?" Kate didn't realise Lucy was standing so close. "About your step father," she replied giving her middle brother a defiant glance.

"Patrick's right Kate, but we will talk after the holiday we have so much to catch up on so let's not spoil the party until after twelfth night.

"What's so special about that apart from the fact all the decorations have to come down etc? I hate it everything looks so bare."

Josephine stretched, looked at the time then suggested she and Aubrey took their offspring and made them ready for bed.

Christina made to get up but Kate noticed her sister-in-law looked more than a little tired, said much to her own surprise, "I'll bath the boys if you get their night things."

"And daddy, we like our daddy to get us ready for bed, he tells us about when he was as little as us." Cameron informed his aunt. "Did you know our daddy when he was a little as us?" added his brother.

"No I didn't." Before Kate could explain came the inevitable "Why."

"Come along kiddos I will explain while I bath you."

Promising to come up and tuck them in Christina lay back in her chair with a sigh.

"I truly love my babies to bits but it's nice to have someone else answer the constant WHY."

CHAPTER 8

While all the excitement was taking place at Pipers Gate, one old lady was having some excitement of her own. Dame Grace Drummond was about to have a caller. No, not a Carol singer, more of an audience. On the stroke of four o'clock on a very cold star bright Christmas Eve her butler opened the front door to her guest, invited him in then taking his coat, hat and scarf informed him Madam would see him in the Parlour.

"Do come in Dr or shall I address you as Professor, you can tell Mrs Russell to bring in the tea things now, thank you." Grace said to the retreating back of her butler.

"Do sit down and draw your chair closer to the fire if you are cold, although I have the central heating turned up full volume at present.

As you know I am the great aunt of Kate McKenzie a young woman for whom I have a great affection. I also do not take kindly to those who choose to make her unhappy. A long time ago at about this time of the year she was let down very badly by one Jamie Tallington, second son of the present Lord Jeremy Tallington. From what I have observed she has taken steps to avoid allowing anybody getting close to her again. Now then young man, from what I saw during the plethora of McKenzie marriages during 1995 you were present at least two of them and from the way you acted towards Kate had me thinking I was about to attend wedding number five.

So will you answer me this?" Before the gentleman sitting opposite her could open his mouth she continued. "Did I or did I not see you kissing her as though it was about to go out of fashion at Sebastian's nuptials? Did Kate kiss you back? Yet again I almost fall over you when Josephine was married to that lovely man Aubrey. What changed between you? I saw her face when you said goodbye before you left for your trip to China. Did it not occur to you to invite her to go with you, as on honeymoon?"

Professor Charles Fitzroy Blossom sat still, he felt as though his senses had run into a battering ram.

"Mrs Drummond I'm not quite sure why I am here. You issued an invitation at short notice, delivered to my parents address in the hope that I might receive it before Christmas. Then you give me a lecture about something private between Miss sorry Dr Katherine McKenzie and myself." He stood up. "I think I should go, but before I do I will tell you briefly what happened between us. In one word nothing. Yes I did love Kate or rather I do, but something happened at Sebastian's wedding. Jamie Tallington who I have known since we were at prep school together explained years ago he and Kate were an item, and he was waiting until she finished at university before they were married, but due to a slight misunderstanding it didn't happen that way. I asked Kate about it but she said she would rather not talk about it. I was literally warned off."

"So young man you allowed a man, who Kate has never spoken to or been in his company for over twelve years warn you off. I'm disappointed in you Professor Blossom I really thought you had more steel in your spine than allow Kate to get away."

Charles Fitzroy Blossom, brilliant scholar, poplar lecturer, well liked by his fellow academics, wondered just what he was doing here on Christmas Eve listening to an elderly relative of one Professor Katherine McKenzie who he loved so much it physically hurt. He rubbed his fist over the area where he thought his heart was. Sitting down again he looked as miserable as he felt.

"Mrs Drummond." before he could continue she butted in.

"How about Great Aunt Grace." as she said it she smiled and as she did so her whole expression changed from that of haughty autocratic to a softer gentle look. "Let me tell you a story, but first let us have some tea it would be a shame to waste it." Handing him as cup she began her tale.

"It was of a love found only to have it snatched from her without her consent, then of another love but not ever quite the same. Late in the autumn years of her life her first love was found, but only for a short time before he died. But let me tell you this when we found each other again, although he was not free to marry, we lived together for almost nine years, and they were the happiest years of my life." Putting her hand over her visitor's gave it a gentle squeeze. "Don't wait until your twilight years before claiming your love Charles."

CHAPTER 9

Professor Charles Fitzroy Blossom prepared to leave Kate's Great Aunt Grace first thanking her for inviting him to tea and then promising her he would think very carefully about what she had said about second chances. He loved Katherine McKenzie with an intensity which had surprised him. He recalled their first meeting, in her twin sister's place of work. Taking part in a project proposed by an eleven year old boy. And a very successful project it turned out to be he recalled with a faint smile. Oh yes Cornelius Patrick Rogers was definitely going places once he finished his education. Turning into his parents driveway Charles thoughts returned to Katherine McKenzie, once the immediate Christmas festivities are over he would go to Pipers Gate and try to explain what had happened and put matter right between them again. No not to put matter's right, to hell with that. He would tell Katherine how much he loved her and hoped in some small way she returned his love. Having settled that thought in his mind he let himself into the house. His parents Doctors Roland and Lola Blossom had left two days ago to go on a cruise for 17days. Charles was staying in their house more or less until they came back.

As he entered the inner hall he was greeted by the strident ringing of the telephone. Lifting the receiver he had just managed to give the phone number when the agitated voice of his sister-in-law cut in.

"Charles, thank goodness you are home can you get over to Ampthill as soon as possible, we have an emergency and I need your help."

"Calm down Lauren, tell me what has happened."

"It is that idiot of a brother of yours he has been in a freak accident, and I'm at the Bedford General A&E waiting while they make up their minds if they are going to operate tonight or leave it until tomorrow."

"Lauren what has Keith done, and how bad is he?"

Charles heard his sister-in-law draw a shuddering breath.

"I that is, they think he has broken his hip and are not quite sure if he has done something to his back."

"Where are the children?"

"My next door neighbour is looking them, but I cannot leave them there, it's Christmas Eve," her voice ended in a sob."Please Charles can you help?"

"Of course I will be right over, which neighbour left or right?"

"Number 7, the house to the right of ours, I must stay with Keith until we know what's going to happen but I will telephone you as soon as I know."

"Lauren, give me a phone number where I can reach you, then I will arrange to take care of the children."

Having ascertained a contact phone number and where to find the children's presents Charles locked his parent's front door and drove as though the devil was on his tail to Ampthill in Bedfordshire

Whoever designed flat-pack toys for children should be horsewhipped Charles muttered to himself. It was now some seven hours since his mercy dash from Suffolk to Bedfordshire. He had collected Jessica aged six going on twenty-six and Steven just four, his birthday was the twentieth of December his sister had informed her uncle at least as many times as his years.

"We were saving his party until Daddy came home; his birthday cake is in the larder. Daddy's plane was delayed so we had to wait." Her voice wobbled but she didn't cry, Charles drew his niece to him and putting his arms round her said, "I know it's hard to be brave but your Daddy will be home with you both as soon as he possibly can. When your Mummy returns from the hospital she will explain what has happened."

All was quiet, Lauren had telephoned and spoken to her children telling them their Daddy had hurt his leg but she would be home before Santa Claus was due to call.

Lauren had arrived home just before mid-night tearful and exhausted. The police constable who had driven her home helped her inside at the same time telling Charles his sister-in-law would be OK once she had something to eat and a rest.

"A lady in her condition should not be sat in A&E for hours on end it wouldn't do her or the baby any good." With a brief salute he wished them both a Merry Christmas and left.

Lauren promptly burst into tears and Charles taking her his arms shushed her as though she was the same age as her daughter.

"Come on love let's get you something to eat then into bed. I didn't know we had another little Blossom on the way, when is the baby due?"

"The end of January, give or take a day or two. Sorry for crying all over you like a water spout but it's been an awful day, and now it's Christmas and Keith is not here."

"Now let's get you that hot drink, I don't suppose you have eaten since you heard about the accident."

"No in the hospital they were very kind but I was so worried I couldn't eat."

"Right here we go then, tea then scrambled egg on toast, will that do, it's easy to eat and sustaining."

Scrubbing her face with a damp tissue Lauren nodded her head.

"Thank you Charles, I'm sorry if I spoiled your plans but I didn't know who else to turn to. My parents have gone off to the wilds of Scotland for the holidays and all of your tribe seem to have gone to the far corners of the earth." This was said with a wobbly smile. "How did you manage at bed time?"

"Jessica helped, she knew exactly what they had for supper and explained to me in great detail that Steven went to bed one hour before her. That was because she is the eldest."

"That's my girl sometimes I feel as though I rely on her more than I should, but with Keith being away for the last two months and me being pregnant she has been a great help."

"Finish up your eggs then bed."

"What about the presents?." "OK if you tell me where they are I will play Santa Claus."Little did Charles know what he was letting himself in for.

Two am on Christmas morning, never in his wildest dreams had Charles Blossom imagined he would be struggling with a flat-pack toy garage. He scanned the drawing again, he checked the pieces again, also the screws to hold the pesky thing together. Right according to the diagram all the necessary items where there, so why in the name of heaven it didn't fit together as it should.

OK one more try, then he would hide the dratted thing away until the child's father came home. Spreading all the main pieces on the dining room table he assembled the finishing pieces to one side then started again. "If it doesn't work this time I've had it. Now then if this piece goes here, that other side should screw into place there." It was at this point Charles realised he had two pieces for the back and no part for the front. Some idiot had not checked this item properly before selling it to some poor unfortunate parent with little or no knowledge of DIY skills.

CHAPTER 10

It was still very dark when two small boys found their way into their parent's bed. "Are you awake?" Cameron's small hand gently lifted his father's eyelid. Sebastian groaned to himself. "If I wasn't I am now."

"Can we come in?" Alistair whispered.

"Shush come with me and see if Santa Claus has been."

"Yes he has but we didn't touch anything like you said until you woke up," whispered Cameron. "Alistair said we had to wait and we did."

"You are waked up now, so we can." put in Alistair.

"Come into bed for a cuddle first."

The children didn't have to be asked twice, they loved their early morning cuddle with their parents; this was how most mornings started in this particular McKenzie household.

Cuddled up between their parents Cameron leaned against his mother and gently stroked her face. He knew she liked this because his Daddy does it, lots of times.

"What time is it love?" Christina opened her eyes she had woken up when her boys clambered into bed but had hoped to catch a few minutes doze before the excitement of the morning really got started.

"Not quite seven ' clock but let's all have a few more minutes before getting up." Sebastian suggested.

"How much is a few minutes?"

"Did anybody ever tell you boys you talk too much?"

"Yes." chorused two voices. Pansy does, she told us we are like Shona; her mummy says she does."

"Does what." enquired their father.

"Talk lots, do you know she has to say lots of words to people." Alistair turned his daddy's face towards him. "She told me."

Shona Douglas had been spotted by a friend of Sebastian when she had acted the part of narrator in the first school Christmas performance. It had gone down in the history of St. Paul's Comprehensive as one of the greatest amateur performances ever. The Rock Nativity had been Christina and Lucy McKenzie's first joint venture. Mr. Hilary Du Bois had sponsored Shona when she had secured a place in the North London School of Dramatic Art where she had taken to it like a duck to water.

"Right my boys, let's get you washed and dressed then breakfast." Sebastian waited just a heartbeat.

"No, dressed, not washed we was washed before bed." two voices rose in protest. This happened every morning and was also a part of the getting up ritual with this small pair. Rolling the little boys over, their daddy tickled them while they shrieked with laughter. After a few minutes Christina put a stop to the laughter from all three males in her bed by getting up and removing herself from the tumbled sheets.

"Come you two let's see what Santa left for you."

"Come Daddy you too." seizing their parents hands they went into the adjoining room where a very large Christmas stocking lay on the end of each bed. The children's main gifts were downstairs under the big tree in the hall where they would remain until after Christmas dinner. when all the fun would start. Sebastian and Christina had exchanged their personal gifts to each other on Christmas Eve.

Finally they joined the rest of the family for breakfast in the main dining-room."From the sound coming from the room it seemed as though Santa had been extraordinarily busy last night," remarked Lucy's sister Fiona, turning to speak to Aubrey.

"Wherever did you manage to get it, I didn't dream in a million years it was possible. Do you know tickets are like gold dust?" She leaned over and gave her adopted brother-in-law a resounding kiss on the cheek. "Dr Jo, did you know what this lovely man of yours has done?"

Shaking her head, "No but as you say this lovely man of mine knows lots of people in the right places. So when is this concert?"

"February 22nd in the Barbican, it's a special charity performance by Nils Bailey, one of the great concert pianists. He has a special music academy in York and only does a concert once in a while. I should have liked to study the violin there but I couldn't get a place. I shouldn't grumble because I was very lucky to have won a place at the University School of Music in Cambridge." Turning her attention to her small honorary nephew sitting in his high-chair asked."Has Santa Claus been to visit you Freddie?" But he was more interested in his breakfast than someone called Santa Claus.

Elizabeth rose to her feet in order to attract everybody's attention.

"If anyone wished to go to church unaccompanied I have arranged for two babysitters to be available. For those of you who wish to stay home, hot mince pies with mulled wine will be served mid-morning in the small dining-room. Christmas Dinner will be served one o'clock clock sharp. After we have eaten everything up and had our faces washed," this was directed at the younger members of the family, "we will open our gifts from under the Christmas Tree."

"Does this include me Aunt Elizabeth.?" Michael Shaw, Lucy's other sibling had a wicked glint in his eyes. "Must I wash my face before opening my presents?" Elizabeth looked at him, how he had altered from a scared and withdrawn teenager of three years ago into this confident smiling young man.

"Yes you too Michael, if you manage to get gravy or Brandy sauce round your mouth." The twins looked suitably impressed. If their uncle Michael had to wash his face first it must be very special after dinner.

Kate decided to go to church with the others, it was a long time since she had attended a Christmas service at home, thirteen years, it seemed another lifetime away. She joined them in the hall together with Heather Wilson.

As everyone paired off with their spouses it was Christopher and Heather who walked with Kate the short distance to the parish church.

"I expect the Tallington tribe will be present but you're safe with us. I won't let Jamie bother you."

"Christopher it's OK I have got over Jamie a long time ago." replied his sister besides what's with you and Sybil Buchanan?

"Nothing we are just friends."

"Christopher if I didn't know you better I would say you telling me porkies."

"Tell you later, in private not a word to Ma promise."

"Promise. Oh my! Just look at that tree, doesn't it look fabulous, somebody knows a thing or two about design."

"That must be the new vicar, she is a great one for getting things done, so long as they are done her way." answered Heather. "But she has pulled this parish around, which is a good thing, and the congregation is increasing."

The Vicar was good, not just good but very good. Laura Featherstone mounted the pulpit, and looked at the assembled congregation. There was a collective hush all waiting for her to begin, this, her first Christmas morning sermon.

"First let me wish you all a very happy and Blessed Christmas. I am sure each and every one of you knows the wonderful story about the Baby Jesus being born in a stable in Bethlehem. However this morning I am going to ask you all to use your imagination and allow me to tell you a very modern version of this wonderful story.

Four years ago some very clever members of the McKenzie family put on a remarkable end of term spectacular performance called the Rock Nativity and with their very kind permission I am going to ask the question this performance asked then."

As Dr Featherstone began to weave the magic of the modern version of the age old story, those in the congregation almost sat on the edge of their seats. Discretely looking at her watch Laura noted it was time to draw the story to a close. "So I ask you once again, the elderly gentleman passing in the street could he have been Joseph?, the lady in the super market wishing the last customer would hurry so she could rest her weary feet, perhaps she was Mary's mother? My Christmas message is hold out your hand in fellowship to the stranger in town or in this case village, don't be too quick to judge, usually there is an explanation why someone is grumpy or brusque. Love thy neighbour as thyself, In the Name of the Father, the Son and the Holy Spirit Amen.

The service was over and as the people gathered outside, Kate saw Jamie Tallington leave his family and hasten towards her. He looked at her as he expected her to bolt as she had on more than one occasion. A look of surprise crossed his handsome face. Kate was actually walking towards him.

"Happy Christmas Jamie." and as he bent to kiss her she stepped back a pace she wasn't ready to get that close, at least not yet.

"Happy Christmas Kate, it's good to see you again. How long are you staying, at Pipers Gate I mean?"

"I'm not sure Jamie, I have several things to do whilst I'm here but I am not returning to the States for at least the next six months." This was the amount of time she was allowing herself to track down one Professor Charles Blossom.

Keeping a smile on her face she asked after his parents, his brothers and sisters together with their offspring. But instead of answering Kate's question Jamie continued without a pause. "Mother tells me all of the family are in residence this year. I cannot imagine Sebastian being a Daddy to twins, and your sister having two little boys."

"It was no surprise to us as you know twins run in the family and there is still Patrick and Lucy not yet parents." responded Kate.

"What about you and Christopher? Anyone on your horizons?

Kate looked about her and with a sardonic smile replied."Oh my goodness my family are going without me, catch up with you sometime bye." and with a whisk of her berry red coat she was gone.

"Kate what was all that about? He didn't upset you did he?"

Placing her hand on her brother's arm, "Let us go home love I cannot wait to see what Santa has brought me. And no Christopher, he didn't upset me I think it was the other way about."

CHAPTER 11

Christmas morning was not so cheerful or for that matter happy for some members of the Blossom family. Bedford Hospital had telephone just after eight o 'clock to advise Mrs Lauren Blossom her husband's condition was giving them some cause for concern and under the circumstances they were having Mr Blossom transferred to the Addenbrooks Neurological Unit for further investigation.

Fortunately Charles had taken the call instead of his sister-in-law. After enquiring if his brother was in any immediate danger the reply was negative but his condition was giving rise for concern as he was not responding to treatment.

"Mr Blossom, is it possible for you to take your sister-in-law directly to Addenbrooks, we are planning to move Dr Blossom within the next half hour by Helicopter."

"Helicopter."! Repeated Charles, " how badly injured is my brother? From the little my sister-in-law told me last night he had had a fall on the platform at their local railway station."

The nurse took a deep breath before replying, "Mr Blossom under normal circumstances we would not divulge the following information to anyone other than the next of kin but seeing how Mrs Blossom is near her delivery date I will tell you and then you can decide what to tell her. Dr Keith Blossom was a victim of what is called a *Steamer Gang*. They regularly rush through a carriage on a moving train robbing the passengers of money and any small valuables they can seize and get off the train at the next station without being caught. Unfortunately such a gang was being chased by the Railway Police when it stopped at the station where a few seconds earlier your brother had alighted and it was as he was about to descend the steps from the bridge going over the track towards the exit this gang ploughed into him knocking him down two flights of stairs. The police think some of them must have trampled on him in their haste to escape which caused the severity of Dr Blossom's injuries."

"Can you give me any indication what injuries my brother has sustained? The reason why I'm asking you is so I can break it to Lauren without alarming her."

It was at this point the lady herself took the phone from Charles and speaking in a low voice so she wouldn't alarm her children said. "Lauren Blossom speaking will you please tell me without the frills exactly what has happened to my husband?"

It was not the nurse who replied but the Doctor who was overseeing the transfer of Keith Blossom on Christmas morning to Addenbrooks Neurological/ Orthopaedic section.

"Mrs Blossom, your husband has a severe back injury; we are not sure how bad the problem is but until he has specialist attention this cannot be addressed. However we, that is, our team, will give it our best shot. I will alert staff nurse to look out for you when you arrive. Facilities can be arranged for you to stay with him until we have completed various tests etc. Should you go into labour everything will be taken care of at our Rosie Maternity Unit. Try not to worry, my name is Dr Lewis and I am going back with Dr Blossom. I came over from Cambridge early this morning to make sure he is fit to travel. See you later."

Handing the receiver back to Charles, Lauren sat down at the same time rubbing her back.

"Charles we are going to have to think this new situation through."

"Before we do anything." interrupted her brother-in-law we are all going to eat a Christmas Morning breakfast."

"Will we like it? Jessica asked with just a hint of anxiety in her voice.

"Will I?" echoed Steve.

"Yes, I am positive you will, we all will." responded Charles.

"How do you know?" young Steve wasn't convinced.

"Because when your Daddy and I were little boys at home much like you, we always had a Christmas Morning breakfast.

"What's a Christmas morning breakfast?" Once again Jessica wanted details.

"OK here goes, crispy fried bacon, one large plump tinned tomato, one fried egg, sunny side up, sprinkled with magic Christmas Dust." Charles waited just a heartbeat for the next question and it wasn't long in coming.

"What does Magic Christmas Dust look like?"

Looking directly towards a silent Lauren, Charles replied "it means you each have one special wish and you breath it into your hand then carefully sprinkle it over your breakfast, but must not tell anyone what it is you wish for, but I will promise before bedtime you will have your wish granted, but," here uncle Charles held up his hand "it has to be something you both want and not something silly like inviting me to tea."

Both children thought for a minute or two, and then the elder child grinned.

"Uncle Charles, you are already here so why should we invite you to tea?" Then a smile lit up her face. "I know what to wish for, come on Steve let's get our Christmas stockings and I will tell you what to wish."

As the children disappeared towards their bedrooms Charles said with a smile,

"Well so much for democracy. Now then Lauren I am going to cook up this Christmas special breakfast and you are going to take a nice warm shower, then after we have seen what Santa has brought for us we are all going on a winter holiday."

Lauren looked at Charles as though she was emerging from a trance.

"What do you mean going on a Winter Holiday?"

"Yes love, I have a perfectly good house in Cambridge almost on the door-step to Addenbrooks, all I have to do is pack up all the presents etc, several changes of clothes, all the Christmas goodies you will have stocked up together with the Christmas Pudd and we are off. I reckon I will have us all tucked in number 5 Sycamore Road before dark. It means we will be having our Christmas Dinner at teatime but that won't matter just this once. And before you get yourself into a state we will drop you off at the hospital as soon as the medical team say you can go. How does that sound?"

Lauren tried very hard to smile at her clever brother-in-law, but the effort was just a tad too much. Charles just held her. Burying her face against his shoulder, Lauren cried for her husband, for herself, her children's disappointment that their daddy wasn't with them and lastly for the man who had given up his own plans to come to her rescue.

Drying her tears, Lauren stepped back, drew herself up saying, "right lets fall in with your brilliant idea. You cook, I shower, we eat, I pack, you collect our possessions, and then we are off, all points east."

All went as planned and it was just after mid after-noon as the winter sun was setting turning the spires of Cambridge into burnished gold that Charles turned into the drive of his home with his own little band of pilgrims.

Just twenty miles further east as the crow flies, one Katherine McKenzie was looking out at the same setting sun and repeating under her breath the pilgrims prayer and directing it towards one Professor Charles Blossom where ever he was, hoping he would somehow pick it up on the ether. "

Charles I think I fell in love with you when we first met, somehow we seem to have lost our way, but hang in there man I am going to find you and never let you out of my sight again."

CHAPTER 12

Christmas night at Pipers Gate began with high tea and ended in high drama. After all the fun of present giving and present opening the small fry were more than ready for their bed by six o'clock and whilst the two sets of parents ably assisted by doting Aunts readied, bathed, fed and settled them down for the night, the remaining adults lazed round the fire in what was referred to as the large drawing-room reminiscing of Christmas's past.

In this Daniel excelled especially when he recounted his time as a teenager. Teddy Boys with their crepe soled shoes, long draped jackets and elaborate hair styles.

"Did you really wear those? Somehow I cannot imagine you wearing something as outlandish as that. Sorry I didn't mean to sound rude, but look at you even when you are not going to the institute you look smart."

"Michael you had better stop now before you fall any further into the hole you have made." laughed his sister Fiona.

"Its' OK Fiona, sometimes it's difficult for the young ones to imagine us oldies having fun, and those days were fun."

Elizabeth quietly left the group for a short while and when she returned she was carrying a large shoe box. Placing it in the middle floor invited those around her to take a few of the items out of the box and guess who they originally belonged to and what they were.

By the time the assortment of people who felt it necessary to put four little people to bed returned they were greeted with howls of laughter.

"Whatever is going on." asked Sebastian, then recognising the box, answered himself. "Ma you've brought out the old memorabilia box, I hope you have taken out all the ones of me as a teenager."

Before his mother could reply Christina unearthed a piece of hair tied with a length of black velvet ribbon. Attached was a small label stating this was taken from one Sebastian McKenzie on his seventeenth birthday. Looking at the head of her husband she noticed although not so short as the present day norm it must have been quite a sight then.

"How long was your hair Sebastian?"She asked with a grin.

"Oh about as long a Josephine's is now."

"No way brother mine, Christina, it was long enough to plait, rather like that chappie on Gardeners Question time."

"Wow, you must have looked quite something in the olden days" remarked Fiona tongue in cheek. With her eyes alight with laughter Fiona Shaw looked across at Sebastian. She remembered kindness and help in sorting out the mess both she and her brother Michael found themselves in way back in 1995. How the McKenzie family had opened their collective arms and taken care of two frightened and confused teenagers. Fiona and Michael were now more or less a part of the McKenzie' family. Their love and respect for Daniel and Elizabeth was absolute.

After about an hour of *all our yesterdays in a box*, time out was called.

"Is anybody hungry." enquired Heather, because if they are, a buffet supper is being laid out in the dining-room for about eight thirty, please help yourselves."

The excitement of the day settled down to a quiet buzz of conversation, and it was shortly before ten when the phone rang and a strange voice asked for Katherine.

"Who is it?" Kate mouthed to Mr Benson.

"I believe she said her name is Grace Drummond, Dr Kate."

For a moment Kate looked blank then taking the receiver from the butler said,

"Aunty Grace what's happened are you alright, are you ill? Wait a minute I will get Dr Jo and Ma." Putting the phone down before her great aunt could reply she hurried off to summon her sister and mother.

"It's great aunt Grace" she said quietly, "there is something wrong."

"Aunt Grace this is Elizabeth how can we help you?"

"Elizabeth, will you please put Kate back on the line it's her I need, urgently!"

"Can't I help you?"

"No Elizabeth you cannot, so for heaven's sake will you do as you are told."

Handing the phone back to her daughter while at the same time wondering had the old dear finally flipped waited to hear why she was insistent that only Kate could help. As she waited she saw Kate's face change colour then frantically searching for a pen and paper.

"Just a minute Aunty Grace I will have to write this down, yes it will only take a minute. Right, you have the correct address? Number 5 Sycamore Road, off Hills Road, Cambridge. Have you got the post code? Never mind I'm sure I will find it. Telephone number 01580 360849 got it. Yes I understand I will leave right away. Yes you ring and let them know I am coming. I should be there in under an hour. Yes it is good it has turned mild not like last year."

Turning to see her mother hovering behind her Kate gestured towards what was known as Grandpa's study.

"Great Aunty Grace, she has just had an urgent telephone call from Charles Blossom. He rang her in desperation, his brother is seriously injured in Addenbrooks and his sister-in-law has gone into premature labour."

"But what has this to do with you?" queried her mother.

"I'm coming to that. Unfortunately all of their immediate family are too far away to help and he has his brother's family at his house in Cambridge. He transported them from Bedfordshire this after-noon. Being a bachelor he is caught between a rock and a hard place, he also has in his care a six and four year old, it's their mother who is having the baby. Great Aunt said he will explain later why he telephoned her in the first place for help. This is more your forte Dr Jo, but our esteemed great aunt said you were entitled to your Christmas break with your little family and being as I was staying here it might as well be me. Where she got the idea from that I would be any use the good Lord only knows. Anyway I had better pack a nightie and toiletries and will telephone you when I arrive and put you all in the picture."

Inside fifteen minutes flat Kate was on her way.

The roads were dry and frost free, and with the moon riding high in the sky, Kate found the first part of the drive towards Cambridge surprisingly relaxing and despite being unfamiliar with the recent road alterations on the outskirts of the city made good time.

Stopping under a street-light to ascertain she was in the correct road, she noted a house just a little to her left lit up like beacon. "Ah this must be number 5" she muttered to herself. Her intuition proved correct. Parking outside on the street in order to leave room for the car on the drive to reverse out if need be, she mounted the three shallow steps and placed her hand on the bell.

Nothing had prepared her for the next step in this rather unusual Christmas night. The letterbox opened and a voice said. "Please give me your name and the house you have come from."

Kate hesitated then hungering down so she could look through the small gap replied; "My name is Dr Katherine McKenzie but my family and friends call me Kate, and I am staying with my mother and family at Pipers Gate in a place called Brackonfield. Now let me guess, you have an uncle called Charles."

"Yes, Professor Charles Fitzroy Blossom."

Kate waited then asked carefully, "is Uncle Charles there with you, or would you like to go get him and tell him Kate is here to help?"

The child stood still for a moments before she replied. "He knew you would come but not quite so quickly, will you stay there while I fetch him. He is with Mummy she is poorly and he didn't want to leave her until someone came."

Then she was gone calling at the top of her voice," Uncle Charles, come and let Kate in she is here just like you said."

Within a matter of seconds the missing Professor Charles Blossom opened the door- almost dragging the woman standing waiting to be admitted, inside.

"Thank God you have come, its Lauren, she thought it was just cramp but she thinks the baby is coming, and it's not supposed to come out for at least another four weeks. I have telephoned the Rosie maternity unit and they said to bring her in and they would check her over, but Lauren says it's too late the baby is nearly here."

Handing Charles her overnight bag Kate said a hasty prayer to whoever might be on hand to listen turned to Charles asking."Where exactly is your sister-in-law now?"

"In my bed, it's a king size and there is more room to move around in. I have plenty of towels and hot water and stuff and." but poor man, he had run out of words.

Entering the room Charles indicated Kate saw the tearful face of the mother to be.

Crossing to the bed she took Lauren's sweating palm in her hand.

Mrs Blossom, can you tell me how far along you are, Charles said you think or rather you know we cannot get you to the hospital in time."

Looking into the calm beautiful face bending over her, Lauren took a shuddering breath. "I have had a back ache all day but I thought it was stress but when I returned from visiting my husband about a couple of hours ago I was bending over bathing Steve, he is my youngest, a little boy, I had this searing pain across the base of my back and everything seemed to happen very fast from then on.

A little while ago just after the Rosie said for me to go in for a check up I felt different and now the baby will be here very soon. I am trying to be brave because I don't want to frighten the children." Just a Lauren finished speaking she started to pant. "Quick the baby is coming now."

Kate realised this was no time for false modesty, she whipped away the blankets and leaving the sheet in place grabbed a large towel from the bottom of the bed and lifting the sheet away from the mother to be placed the towel under her knees just in time to take hold of the newest addition to the Blossom family.

Looking frantically about her for something to tie the umbilical cord, Charles appeared at her side and handed Kate a piece fresh string and a pair of scissors

"I boiled the scissors and the string just in case we didn't make the hospital in time." he said a little sheepishly.

Kate did what she hoped was the necessary and after wrapping the new born infant up in a smaller towel handed it to his mother.

"Well Kate, are you going to tell what we have, a nephew or a niece?"

Kate looked blank. "Eh! I don't know in all the excitement I forgot to look."

"Its' OK Charles." a voice full of tired laughter spoke from the bed. "Keith and I have another little boy."

It was at this moment a siren was heard coming near and nearer.

"I think this must be the ambulance, I telephoned the hospital soon as you arrived just in case we got into difficulties. But ladies we all did just fine."

Two pair of eyes speared the only grown up male present.

"Charles Blossom, may I suggest you have the next Blossom baby while we, that is, Kate and me watch." But whatever Lauren was about to say next was left unsaid. The Paramedics took over and in no time at all the new mother and baby were whisked away with the promise they would be back just as soon as they were both checked out.

It was almost an anticlimax; Kate was left to reassure Jessica that her mummy and new baby brother would be back with them very soon. Charles elected to make some sandwiches and hot chocolate then hopefully have a good night's sleep.

Looking at her watch Kate was surprised to see it was almost one a.m. in the morning, too late to start for home now besides how could she leave Charles on his own with two young children missing their mummy?

She also wanted to hear the full story from start to finish about his brother and how the family ended up here in Cambridge, and finally how come her great aunt had become involved. If she didn't know better she thought it was a great big conspiracy brought about by the gods of her father to get her and Charles back together again. Trying to suppress a yawn Kate was conscious of someone taking her empty cup from her hand.

"Come along my favourite princess let me show you to your room, I've put a hot-water bottle in your bed, we will talk in the morning."

CHAPTER 13

Kate opened her eyes one at a time, something was wrong, the window was in the wrong place and someone had changed the curtains during the night. Slowly her memory returned, and just as she was about to get out of bed to check if anyone was up and about she saw the door open just a little at first, then enough for a small boy with a thatch of red-gold curly hair to peep inside.

"Hello, I'm Kate and you must be, let me guess Steve who is now four. Would you like to come right inside?"

Holding out her hand Kate invited him to sit on the bed beside her. "Does your mummy give you a good morning cuddle, mine does even when I am all grown up? She says, my Mum, it's the best start to the day."

"My Daddy has hurt his leg, and he missed my birthday." The child's eyes filled with tears, "but as soon as he is better we will have it then."

Still not coming any further into the room he continued; "Mummy said we must not talk to strangers and if they frighten us we have run and scream very loudly."

"I understand Steve and of course you don't know me because I arrived very late last night after you had gone to sleep. So if you go and find your uncle Charles and let him know I am getting up then he can tell you who I am, and how I came to be here in bed in your uncle's house."

Looking at Kate with blue eyes as big as saucers he laughed calling as he went to find his uncle."Uncle Charles can you come quickly, we have a Goldilocks in your bed and I found her first."

Professor Blossom required no second invitation, taking the stairs two at a time arrived at Kate's bedroom door to be greeted by an excited little boy.

"She said to tell you, you will tell me, how she is in your bed, just like Goldilocks in the Three Bears."

"No she isn't, Goldilocks has yellow hair, this lady looks like Snow White; she has black hair, and very dark eyes and lovely skin. I know because when I was five, Daddy took me to see a Pantomime in London."

Advancing to the bedside the petite figure of a girl about five or six with the same hair colouring as her brother but sapphire blue eyes under slightly arched black eyebrows

My goodness this young lady is going to be a raving beauty by the time she is grown up. Heaven help the local male population. Bringing her mind back to the present Kate once again introduced herself.

"You must be Jessica, how do you do." The little girl smiled, the formal introduction was not lost on her.

"Now we have all introduced ourselves it's time for breakfast in about fifteen minutes. See you downstairs Kate, oh yes before I forget there are plenty of towels in your bathroom and." Charles paused then with a wide grin continued, "Mother and baby are both doing well. In little while I will phone the hospital and ask if we can go in and see your new baby brother

In all the excitement no one asked if Kate was going go with them to the hospital, so it was a complete surprise when Charles asked why she wasn't ready to go.

"We are ready, faces washed and teeth cleaned." called Jessica.

"Good, so off you go, your Uncle Charles is outside in the car waiting for you."

"You have to kiss us goodbye and tell us to be good." admonished Jessica, "it is what mummy does, even says it to daddy when he goes away."

Kate felt herself tear up. "Goodbye darlings enjoy your visit and be good." It nearly finished her off when both children lifted their faces for a goodbye kiss.

"Hold it right there Princess, you missed me out." Charles literally bounded up the steps and throwing his arms around Kate's middle kissed her hard on the mouth.

Stepping back from one very startled lady Charles put his hand very gently under her chin. "Wait for me Princess I will be back as soon as I can. I do not intend to stay very long then perhaps we can all visit later this afternoon."

Kate stood mute she didn't dare open her mouth in case she burst out crying, so she just stood there and simply nodded her head.

Watching the car drive out of the road she went back inside and viewed the wreckage in the kitchen.

Every surface was littered with goodness knows what. Dirty dishes in the sink, the draining board had several large saucepans stacked up, whatever had they been used for. Breakfast had consisted of scrambled eggs, bacon and baked beans. And she was sure she had only used one skillet.

"Clean the work surfaces first, and then stack the dishwasher next. Then wash the floor, no telephone Ma." Kate found she was talking to herself. God! It's the first sign of insanity. Picking up the phone she called Pipers Gate. The phone was immediately picked by Christopher. "Kate! Where the devil are you? We are all worried sick we haven't heard a word from you since Christmas night. Ma has been imagining all manner of things."

"Hold on little brother I have lots to explain, but be patient and I will tell you what happened then we will have and 'Q and A' session later."

Kate explained in detail the adventure of the previous night and the more recent happening of the morning. Christopher relayed the story a piece at a time as Kate was speaking thus bringing her family up to date. The first question came from her mother.

"Kate have you definitely promised to wait until they all return from Addenbrookes?" "The short answer is yes, next question."

"How are you managing? You will need a further change of clothes plus some things for the newborn, any idea of baby's weight or size?"

"Josephine you are an angel, will you ask Heather if she will pack me enough things for at least a week, even if Lauren is sent home tomorrow I cannot leave them on their own and Charles will want to visit his brother, as for the new born I'm sorry I haven't a clue, all I remember it was red, very slippery and sort of screwed up a bit, not like Freddie or Oliver."

Her sister laughed.

"Kate when you saw your nephews for the very first time they were almost four weeks old, the brand new looks goes of very quickly. Anyway, until someone can go to Bedfordshire and collect Lauren's things I will telephone home and ask if either Miriam or Mrs Brice will pack some of Freddy's first size baby grows etc. then when Charles gets back perhaps you or he can drop by Church House and collect them." Kate could hear a muffled conversation going on in the background then her Ma came back on the phone.

"Kate problem solved Christopher has very kindly offered to bring your fresh clothes etc. and will call at Church House to pick up whatever you need. In the meantime it is very obvious Charles will not have much in by the way of food so will you please make an inventory of the fridge and freezer then Christopher will bring enough food to last you for the rest of the week."

After thanking her mother for her generosity Kate hung up. Now what, looking at her watch she yelped one thirty already where had the day gone, soon it would be New Years Eve.

Did she want to be stuck in the Cambridge suburbs instead of dancing the night away with friends then finishing up at her sister and brother-in-law's house? Glancing about her in the now pristine looking kitchen she put all thoughts of partying out of her mind. She had better start checking fridge and freezer before Christopher set off on his self imposed rescue mission. Ten minutes later she was back on the phone to Pipers Gate. It was Heather who answered her this time.

"Right my girl, let's have your list. As Kate relayed the items she needed, Heather cut in a couple of times with very welcome advice regarding food for small people.

"Heather you are an angel and I will be forever in your debt. Would you happen to have one of your special Victoria Sponges in the freezer, you know one where all you have to do is wait until it defrosts then eat it all before the cream goes off."

"Yes I will pack it in a box by itself so be careful and don't let Christopher cut what he calls a slice, that will mean nearly half, and oh before I forget, I have also packed one of my Corn- Beef Hash pies, it will do for your evening meal tonight, and I have packed fresh veg just in case your Professor Blossom has overlooked them, it's surprising how men overlook vegetables."

As she waited for the Blossom family to return Kate decided to explore the rest of the house. She suddenly realised she had only seen two bedrooms and the kitchen so far. She looked into the lounge first, a good sized room with minimum amount of furniture, two sofas, in pale grey leather, one desk under the window, two bookcases one either side of the fireplace. A couple of free standing lamps and what looked to be a very complex music centre behind one of the sofa's. This is definitely a man's room. No photographs, no pictures with exception of what appeared to be a very old map of the world behind glass hanging over the mantel shelf.

The dining-room was equally austere, a long sideboard, one long dining-table and eight chairs, with yet another book case but this one stretching the full height and width of the wall immediately behind the door. The only items to redeem the room from being dull and dreary were the curtains which were vibrantly coloured silk, full and lush, and a startlingly beautiful glass chandelier hanging from the ceiling in the centre of the room.

"My! This has the wow factor straight up." Kate murmured. Passing though the hall on her way upstairs, she noticed an excellent Sheraton Hall Table, covered in dust. Mentally putting that on her list of to do tomorrow, she continued on her way. Four bedrooms, the one belonging to Charles which had been used last evening, the bed had been stripped but not yet made up with clean bed linen, Before going down stairs she would check to look for fresh sheets, pillowcases and towels. The other bedrooms were neat and tidy, good that would save time later on, although the one with bunk beds had the remnants of the Christmas wrappings from yesterday. Was it really only one day since Christmas morning mused Kate?

Her thoughts were interrupted by the sound of the front door bell. A pleasant sound not unlike the Westminster Chimes of the Grandfather Clock which stood in the hall at Pipers Gate. Opening the door she was delighted to find her brother.

"Here take this before I drop it; Heather seems to think you are stocking up for a siege." Handing Kate what looked to be a very large hamper like bag. She turned to go back into the kitchen when out of the corner of her eye she saw a large family size car pull up immediately behind Christopher's sports car.

"What on earth is going on? A familiar voice inquired.

"Aubrey what are you doing here? I'm so pleased to see you both."

"I'm on a mission of mercy; my lady wife decided it would be better if I went directly to Church House with a list of things she reckons are absolutely essential for a new arrival." With that throw away remark her brother-in-law produced a very large parcel and asked if he may bring it inside.

"Good idea, if we stand on the doorstep much longer every neighbour in the street will be phoning the local police station."

"Of course both of you come inside, I don't suppose Charles and the children will be long and I'm sure he will want to say thank you."

"Here take the rest of the stuff Heather sent." Handing Kate a medium size grip continued; "if you need any more just give her a ring and she will bring them down for you." Christopher grinned at his sister.

"One more item or rather several more, Gordon sent this lot together with a very posh wreath, I think, from our front door at Pipers Gate."

Kate almost yelped when she saw the amount of greenery, but asked Christopher to say thank you to all those who had pitched in to help.

"Oh yes and when you have a spare minute or two, telephone your Great Aunt to find out why she thought of you to act as the Angel of Mercy."

Giving his Brother-in-Law a slap on the arm called, "OK Judge it's time to get rolling we have to be home before dark," and with that throw away remark gave his sister a hug then hurried out to his car. Aubrey was just about to do the same when a small bundle shot indoors crying out, "leave her alone; she is our Aunty Kate and she is going to live here until our mummy comes home with our new baby brother."

This was said almost in one breath as young Steve Blossom staked his claim to Kate.

Charles followed him indoors with Jessica holding on to his hand.

Aubrey Page just grinned at Charles and holding out his hand saying, "Happy Christmas Charles; it's good to see you home safe and well. You had us worried for a time but now you are home again all will be well. But we will play catch up later." so giving a wave of his hand Aubrey left to return to Suffolk.

At first Charles couldn't take in what Aubrey meant. Who had been worried and who was so pleased to see him again? Putting these questions to one side he would think about them later.

Charles entered his own house to find in his absence Kate had miraculously transformed the hall, his lounge and best of all the kitchen .She had asked if Heather would send something down to Cambridge to make the house a little more festive and Heather had not failed her. One large festive wreath to hang on the front door, several thick strands of tinsel to drape over the mantle shelf in both main rooms and Gordon Brice had sent several large branches of assorted greenery to put into vases. Kate had even used a very ornate umbrella stand in the hall to stash some of the green boughs. It certainly looked and smelled a lot different from when Charles had left for the hospital.

"I hope you are all very hungry."

Steve was still hanging onto her leg. "I am I like my dinner; we only had some crisps and biscuits."

"Uncle Charles didn't have anything," broke in Jessica."He said he wasn't hungry, but I think it was just an excuse. The canteen was closed and the Burger King shop was closed until tea time. He said we would have to wait until we got home."

"Aunty Kate, can you cook? Uncle Charles said you." but whatever Jessica was about to say was cut off at source.

"I think we should all wash our hands before tea then ask Aunty Kate if there is anything we can do to help. I will do bathroom duty, and thank you Kate, for everything." Charles smiled over his shoulder as he ushered the children towards the bathroom.

Sitting back replete with two helpings of pie plus vegetables Charles felt all was right in his world, apart from the fact both his brother and sister-in-law were at present in hospital.

"Have you all had sufficient to eat?" Kate looked at the three faces sitting round the kitchen table.

"Has anyone any room for pudding? I have made two puddings so you have a choice." Kate waited; when they were young and all at home it was an absolute cert that someone would say both. Sebastian usually suggested he would have both his puddings on the same plate to save the washing-up.

"What kind are they?" Jessica wanted to know.

"One is Christmas pudding with brandy sauce or custard and the other is a giant trifle." Charles caught her eye and started to laugh.

"Oh you are a wicked woman, both are my favourites. May I have one large helping of Christmas pudding and two very large helpings of trifle, but not together?"

His niece turned round in her chair and placed her hand on his tummy.

"Uncle Charles, are you quite sure? You had a very big supper, and two big lots of pudding, will you have enough room?"

"You are quite right poppet, but I was going to suggest I had the second pudding later on after you two were in bed. I am going to help Aunty Kate to clear up and you two can watch the television for one hour then its bed for you both."

"UNCLE CHARLES you know I go bed later than Steve because I am older than him."

"Yes Jessica I am aware of that, but last night you went to bed very late for a little girl, so I think an early night will do you no harm."

"That's what mummy says" she replied in a sulky voice, but fortunately did not argue any further.

Charles volunteered to clear up but Kate would have none of it.

"Charles sit down and rest for a while, after I have cleared up I will get the children ready for bed then you can tell me all about your hospital visit."

So suiting actions to words she served the puddings, and then chased the children and one uncle into the lounge to watch television.

CHAPTER 14

Some three hours later Kate decided to call it a day. Children in bed both fast asleep, Charles idly playing with the television remote without much interest in what was actually on offer.

"Charles would you like a drink of," what she wondered? There was no evidence of any kind of alcohol as she had found her way around the kitchen.

Instead of replying Charles held out his hand, "come and sit by me for a while, we have much to talk about."

Taking a seat opposite him Kate sat prepared to listen as she had promised earlier.

"No Kate, beside me right here," patting the seat on his left. Crossing over she did as she was asked and waited.

"Kate before I tell you all that has happened since my SOS to your great aunt or rather my meeting with that august lady, I must tell you I have loved you since that very first time I met you. It was and still is, the most wonderful day in my memory.

I had already met your sister and her future husband, together with her colleagues, and the remarkable Cornelius Rogers. But none of those compared to meeting you, Dr Katherine McKenzie. I had read about your work, and admired your stance against the continued encroachment of land belonging to the indigenous people on this planet of ours. Dr Jo very kindly gave me a copy of *The Pilgrims Prayer*. I had it framed and took it on my travels, to remind me to tread carefully on other people's lives and dreams."

Taking her hand in between his he turned to look directly into her face.

"I am going start at what was to have been the beginning of my dream for us.

"Shush." he murmured. "Let me tell it in my own words. I had intended to tell you about the invitation I received from the Royal Society to take part in an expedition to China to look for rare plants. This was the first invitation to a team of Botanists from the West since the end of the Second World War. It would mean the best part of a year but I knew I could not go without you." Kate could feel his hands on her arms. "No I would not go without you."

Once again Charles stopped, taking a deep breath continued, "I bought this when we were together in Manhattan, that time before I allowed myself to doubt." Letting go of her hand he reached behind him and taking her hand once more said. "Dr Catherine McKenzie before I make a complete fool of myself and weep, will you take this with all my love and marry me. Please!?

Looking down Kate very carefully let go of his hand and handed the small box back to him.

"Will you put it on please?" Silver blue eyes met sloe dark ones and without speaking Charles slipped the simple band of gold mounted with a Sapphire flanked by a Diamond on either side on her third finger.

Placing the palm of her hand against his face Kate gently asked; "What happened Charles? Who spoiled it for you?"

"Lord Jeremy Tallington, he took me to one-side at Sebastian and Christina's wedding reception, and explained you and Jamie had been practically engaged, but you had had a misunderstanding and had flounced off in a huff before Jamie could explain things and put them right between you. And because you wouldn't allow Jamie anywhere near you, the quarrel went on for years. Then when I asked you at Dr Jo's wedding you wouldn't talk to me about it. So I did as Lord Tallington asked me.

I had so desperately wanted you to accompany me to China, but then you told me you had promised to do another two semesters in New York, and would see me if I was still interested when I next visited America."

The silence lasted perhaps three to four minutes then still holding on to her hand Charles felt Kate rather than heard her speak.

"I will tell you what happened all those years ago but first I will make you a promise.

I love you very much; I think I fell in love with you when you told the story about your Grandfather, what a resourceful man he proved to be. Yes Charles I will marry you." She paused, "on condition wherever your travels take you I go with you and when the babies arrive they tag along too."

"All of them." Charles very nearly squawked, but stopped himself in time. "I would not have it otherwise, besides the babies will most likely arrive one at a time." he said this more with hope than certainty. Kate choked on a laugh, "don't bet on it love some of the latest batch didn't."

Drawing her closer to him if that was possible Charles brought his lips to Kate's "I love you Katherine now and forever, now will you have a brandy to celebrate our betrothal?" Kate simply nodded.

Taking a bottle of Brandy from the sideboard plus two balloon glasses Charles came back to the sofa and after handing a glass to Kate raised his in salute, "To us from this day forward wherever we go it is always together."

Taking a sip Kate knew it was time to explain what had taken place to make her turn her back on Brackonfield for so many years.

"Charles it's time to clear up any misunderstandings or suspicion about Jamie Tallington and myself." Making herself comfortable in the circle of Charles arm she began.

"I had just finished my first Michaelmas term at university and was looking forward to Christmas immensely. Jamie Tallington had met me at the station and had promised me a surprise, but I had to wait until the day after Boxing Day. The reason for this was because everybody would be excited and it would be better if there was just the two of us. He wouldn't even let me guess. "I want it to be a surprise for the family but you must know first."

After lunch on the 27th Dec 1984 I set of full of hope. Jamie knew I had loved him all my life, he played with me, taught me to swim, to play tennis, he even took me to a very posh golf club once just for the fun of it. When I was fifteen I told him I loved him and foolishly said we would get married once my education was complete. Jamie said it would be better if I got my degree first then we could work together in the family business. That is one of the reasons I chose Environmental Engineering, before going on to do my Ph.D. in Bio- Diversity, but that would come later.

So there was I, all of nineteen years old, busting with life and expectation. Was Jamie going to tell me he loved me and would wait until I caught him up? Did I tell you he is same age as Christopher? Anyway it didn't matter in the end.

I had been almost one of the Tallington's family for so many years, and had had the run of the place the same as the Tallington boys had Pipers Gate, so it never occurred to me to ask if I could speak to Jamie., I did what I had always done, knocked on the door of his apartment and walked in. I knew if Jamie wanted privacy he always locked the door, so I wasn't expecting anything untoward when I just walked in.

He wasn't in his sitting room I then heard a laugh from his bedroom. It was a laugh I recognised, it sounded like Joshua's fiancé, then I heard Jamie say." Kate felt herself starting to blush from her feet up. "What did he say?" Charles quietly prompted her,

"I heard Jamie say something about young Kate expected later on. Then oh! Bloody hell it must be her. Here get your clothes on while I see to her. The next thing I know Jamie walked out of his bedroom into his sitting-room wearing only his jeans trying to fasten them up as he came towards me.

"Kate what are you doing here? I thought you would have joined the rest of the family."

"I just stood there waiting, then he tried to take my hand, at the same time telling me a Christmas Kiss had got out of hand, it didn't mean anything, it was just one of those things."

I asked him what Joshua would say when found out his fiancé and his brother have been to bed together. Then Alexi came in wearing only her bra and pants. And before Jamie said anything further she laughed and said "Jamie should tell me how he and she had been lovers for simply ages. Joshua wasn't much good in that particular department."

"Can you possibly imagine what I felt like, standing before someone I had worshipped and loved as well as a dear friend, and all he could say was, "these things happen."

"I remember running home as I thought my world had come to an end. I couldn't tell my family what had happened because Alexi Kennedy was engaged to marry Joshua Jamie's elder brother. I went back to university and afterwards put as much distance as I could between the Tallington family and me as possible. About three years later I received an invite to Joshua's wedding, but he didn't marry Alexi it was someone else. I cannot remember her name but she was not a local lady. I thought perhaps Jamie married Alexi when the dust settled. This was one of my reasons why I couldn't come home. I could not meet his wife, Jamie had promised me we would get married when I grew up. He broke his promise. If he had changed his mind about me he should have been honest and told me face to face. That is the reason is why I cannot forgive him."

For a few moments the only sound in the room was that of the fire. Then Charles, pulling Kate closer to his side whispered. "He lost something of great value, something so precious he will regret his callous behaviour for the rest of his life. He didn't marry anyone Kate. I know because the same female came sniffing around Keith but he was not available, he had just finished his PhD in Biotechnology in Geology, and was about to depart for Chile on his first job. Fortunately, before the glamorous Lady Alexi could turn her attention to the remaining Blossom males, our mother had a word with her parents. I don't know what mother said but Alexi left the district not long afterwards."

Turning her face slightly she looked up into his face.

"Your mother's instinct was spot on Alexi Kennedy was not a nice person, she was trouble on legs according to Patrick and he should know." This latest remark was said with such disdain it made Charles smile

"I hadn't seen or spoken to any of the Tallington family for many years until I came home for Patrick's wedding, and Lord Tallington cornered me as he was leaving for home telling me Jamie was still very upset and wanted to put things right. It was all a mistake and he was doing a good turn for some one. He didn't say who, I have no idea what tale Jamie told his parents but it could not have been the truth.

When you stopped talking to me I realised no matter what the problem, I was going to find you and ask WHY? I knew I loved you and I thought you loved me and I couldn't let it go. That is why I came home just before Christmas. I had given myself six months to find you, so here I am."

"No sweetheart it's here we are," finished Charles.

CHAPTER 15

SUNDAY 27TH DECEMBER 1998

The weather was still bright and just a little fresher than it had been over the last two days. Looking round the breakfast table Daniel decided upon a course of action which would put some roses in cheeks and a sparkle in the eye. Waiting until there was a lull in the conversations he rose to his feet.

"Ladies, Gentlemen, Children, I have a suggestion to make which may be of interest to all here present. It is a lovely morning, much too nice to stay indoors, so I am planning on a village walk, Mums and Dads, Grandma and Grandpa, plus of course, all the young people some a quite a bit younger than others. We have Buggies, for little ones, and Backpacks, together with all kinds of things to keep us all warm and cosy on this here village walk. May I have a show hands who are interested, but."! Holding up his large hand Daniel continued, "No one is excluded unless you have some kind of contagious illness, such as lazeitus or a dose of Black Death. Of course I have a cure for the former it's called doing all the washing up from breakfast without the help of the dishwasher." Daniel waited all of sixty seconds. "Good I will meet you all in front of the house in thirty minutes."

"Grandpa, Teddy Edward would like to come too, so would my Aussie bear."

"That can be arranged boys, now scat, I have to wash my face and brush my teeth."

"Well done love, you sound as though you have been a Grandpa for years."

"I think I am trying to make up for lost time Elizabeth. Do you think I'm overdoing the grandpa thing? I decided to arrange a surprise earlier in December when I spotted a poster in the church porch. It advertised a special service in Lavenham church, followed by seasonal attractions all geared for children and adults.

There are no costs involved but, if the grownups are prepared to leave a donation towards a worthwhile charity, Save the Children fund, the organisers will be grateful. I have also taken the liberty of arranging suitable transport."

"No you darling man, you are making the best of now, the time children remember when they become Dads and dare I say Grandpas. Take the now with both hands, hold it close and enjoy."

"Elizabeth, how come you are so wise?" Turning to her Daniel closed his arms around his wife just holding her, simply enjoying the feel of her in his arms. Then dropping a swift kiss upon her mouth said "come along love, we have less than twenty minutes to get ready before the great trek."

"Are we all present and correct?" Daniel counted heads and nodded, good ten adults and four small fry. Let's get going our transport awaits us." With a flourish Daniel swung the Large Oak Front door open, and standing outside was a very plush Mini-bus with the engine running.

"All ready for our village trek. OK then all aboard. The little ones car seats are already in place beside their parents. Pass down the bus please so we can get going."

"I thought we were going on a hike through the village." remarked Lucy. Before Daniel could reply the driver spoke up.

"Good morning everybody today we are going for a village hike round Lavenham

The first stop will be at the Parish Church. At 11.00 am there is to be a children's service of Carols and stories, mostly aimed at preschoolers. There will pop-up books with pictures and some with sounds of farmyard animals. There will be some real live animals present but all secure so no child will be at risk. Afterwards we have booked a table in the Angel Hotel in a private dining room and immediately after lunch there is a Pantomime in the Moot Hall. This lasts just over the hour, and then there is after-noon teas served by all the characters from Alice in Wonderland. We shall be home before dark, so I hope you all will enjoy your day."

Aubrey squeezed Josephine's hand, "Do you remember bringing me here the first time? Its where I knew without a shadow of a doubt how much very I loved you and wanted to marry you without any further delay, but I couldn't begin to tell you because it was just a few days before Patrick and his Lucy were to be married."

Returning the pressure of their joined hands Josephine lifted them to her mouth and gently almost reverently kissed them. "Yes sweetheart, and I was terrified you would see how I felt about you just by looking at me. I was frightened in case I was reading too much into our budding relationship, when all I wanted to do was for you to take me into your arms and make mad passionate love to me."

Aubrey turned his gaze to the face of his wife. "If you continue to look at me as you are now my love I will have to get us off this bus and forget the village hike."

"Until tonight my Lord Judge." she replied with teasing smile.

"Will this be a first time for you Christina?" enquired her cousin.

"Yes Sebastian had said we were going to pay a visit, but lots of things seemed to happen at once so we had to put off going. Aubrey talked a great deal about it when Josephine took him just before your wedding, then it was your Ma and Daniels, then ours."

"Then we found we were expecting a New Year baby." Christina said with a smile directed to her husband.

Bending his head Sebastian buzzed his lips across the mouth of his wife.

"Babies sweetheart and can you remember how thrilled and very proud I was? The lady of my dreams was really and truly my wife, and when the doctor told us we had two babies coming I wanted to stand on the roof and shout so all the world could hear."

"I know love, same with me."

Patrick and Lucy sat hand in hand, they had travelled a different path, together they had faced fear, trauma and hope and now they had another secret, but it would keep until New Year's Day. At present they hugged it to themselves, in their own world of a deep abiding love for each other.

"Daniel, when did you arrange this lovely surprise? It's a wonderful idea, I always found the day after Boxing Day a little flat. Oh I know most people take the next few days to clear up after the Christmas holiday ready for the New Year. But a mystery outing, my dear I think you have hit the Jackpot this time."

Daniel smiled at his daughter -in-law Lucy, "Just enjoy your day my lovely."

CHAPTER 16

While the main contingent of residents of Pipers Gate were enjoying a jaunt round the rural lanes of Suffolk, Christopher had intended to have a leisurely breakfast before going into Cambridge to see if Charles Blossom had any further news about his Brother Keith's condition.

Patrick had mentioned he knew of someone who had suffered an injury to his back due to a motor-cycle accident.

"It's The Reverent Ross Baileys brother-in-law. Speak to Charles or Mrs Blossom about his brother's injury and if it would help I can contact Ross and request his help in making contact," Patrick had suggested.

"We are not returning to London until 4th January, so I shall be about until Addenbrookes make up their minds what if anything they can do, depending on the seriousness of the initial injury.

Daniel intends to have us all home no later than four thirty. Patrick turned towards the door, hesitated then half turning back to his brother asked "Are you going to the Buchanan's before New Year?"

"No, circumstances have changed somewhat, John Buchanan I imagine is going as arranged on the 30th. I am not sure if Sybil will accompany him. I hope to be joining Aubrey and Josephine no later than the 30th as promised, but;" here Christopher hesitated. "Patrick there is no Sybil and Christopher on the cards, it's over."

"But you will definitely be with Josephine and Aubrey before the 31st."

"Yes Patrick, I promise, so away you go, take your lovely wife and show her the hidden treasures Suffolk."

Heather came into the little dining room and sat down next to Christopher.

"Well love I take it you have something else on your agenda this morning," at the same time handing him some more hot toast.

"Yes I'm going to visit Kate and see what is happening there. Would you like to come with me? And you can give me the low down on all that has been happening in deepest darkest Suffolk since my last long visit."

"Thank you Christopher I should like that very much. It will also give me an opportunity to see how Kate and Professor Blossom are managing."

"Heather! You surprise me I'm sure they are managing the children very well, plus of course fitting in visits to the hospital to see the Mummy and new baby and one injured Daddy. Did you ever find out why our revered Great Aunt insisted Kate go on Christmas night?"

"No and neither did your Ma when she telephoned the next morning. All she got was her Aunt's answering machine."

"So can you be ready to leave about eleven thirty?"

"Yes all I have to do is make sure everything is in order for this evening's meal, but Mr Benson is more than capable of making sure all will run like clockwork. It seems a long while since I had a day gallivanting about with such a handsome young man."

The year 1998 was almost at an end but the fates or gods call it what you like, had more shocks in store for the collective McKenzie Family.

Christopher and Heather had left on time, and barely thirty minutes later Mr Benson took a telephone call from Jim Harris butler/bodyguard to McKenzie S.I Ltd.

Mr Benson knew Jim through his association with Professor Daniel and Elizabeth McKenzie Gibson. Mr Benson ran the Gibson household when his employers lived in London and travelled to Pipers Gate when they returned to their country home for any protracted length of time such as now.

"Mr Benson I need to speak to Mr Sebastian." Explaining Sebastian and the family were out and would not be returning much before late after-noon asked could he take a message.

Jim Harris had been with McKenzie S.I. Ltd since Sebastian had started out on his own and was the epitome of discretion but sometime speed was of the essence.

"Mr Benson this message must be given to Mr Sebastian only, not any other member of the household. It is a very delicate and dangerous ongoing matter. The message is as follows. A Dr and Mrs Walsh came earlier today asking for Mr Sebastian. They said they had been given his name together with this address by Mrs Walsh's brother a Mr Aidan Forsythe formerly of Dublin Eire. I told them he was not at home and would not be returning from holiday until the 4th January 1999.

That part was bad enough, I asked if I could take a message or perhaps their telephone number but Mrs Walsh just sort of smiled and said, oh not to bother we might just go down Suffolk and give him a surprise. As they turned to go down the steps I heard Dr Walsh say "why did you open your big mouth. That doorkeeper fellow, holding the door will lose no time in letting him know about our visit without you suggesting we might just go down to Suffolk."

"Mr Harris would you say these people are not, shall we say close friends of Mr Sebastian?"

"You've got it in one Mr Benson, in my previous life I would suggest they skate along just inside the law. One other thing, the woman Mrs Walsh vaguely reminded me of Mrs Lucy, nothing like as pretty, but I think Mrs Walsh could have been quite a looker in her younger days. This pair, are trouble with a capital T, I would bet my life on it. Just make sure there is no one listening when you pass on this message.

Enjoy the rest of your Christmas." and with those closing words Jim Harris hung up.

Mr Benson decided he would write the message down but would keep it on his person until he could get Mr Sebastian on his own, and the best time was after he had finished reading his little boys their bedtime story. Christina usually left her three boys together at story time and joined the rest of the family in the drawing room before dinner. He knew he could rely on Heather to oversee the final preparations thus leaving him time to waylay Mr Sebastian before he went downstairs to join his wife.

CHAPTER 17

It was a very surprised Professor Blossom who opened his front door just after mid-day, to find two people who he least expected.

"Happy Christmas Heather, do please come in Kate will be pleased to see you both." Ushering in his unexpected guests, "I hope you don't mind coming through into the kitchen, we are all in there."

At first the room looked to be full of people but while Charles was taking Heather and Christopher's outdoor coats etc, Heather had time to do a quick count.

Three were female, one of whom was Kate and two men. One of the men looked rather like the woman who was sitting holding a very small baby, next to two young children. These must be the Niece and Nephew of Charles.

Charles, speaking directly to the lady sitting with infant said with a smile in his voice;

"Lauren, let me introduce you to Mrs Heather Wilson, to whom I owe a debt of gratitude, it is she who sent all the goodies with Kate's brother Christopher, which are in the fridge and freezer.

This is Lauren with latest addition to the Blossom family Hugo Charles, and this gentleman is her brother Simon Young. Heather could see the likeness between brother and sister, both had the same red/gold curly hair and eyes almost coloured navy blue.

While exchanging hands-shakes, Christopher was aware brother Simon was looking at Kate as though he would very much like to add her to his lunch menu.

Then taking another look at Kate saw the same expression on her face as he had seen on both his brothers and youngest sister's face very recently. It said loud and clear keep of the grass I'm already spoken for. So Charles and Kate had sorted out their love lives, good that's one problem settled.

Charles completed the introductions, explaining the remaining pair are the police officers who wanted to know how Keith was.

"We have taken one statement from your husband Mrs Blossom, but before we go back to Addenbrookes is there anything you can tell us after you spoke to him last evening?"

"We didn't talk much about the accident we spent most of our time talking about mundane matters, such as how was I going to manage with two small children and a new born, how long he expected to be in hospital.

There was something he said about falling onto his knees at the top of the stairs and being pushed forward, and then somebody jumped on his back and kicked him in the head. The doctors are going to do another CT scan this morning to check for head injuries which may be causing the problem with his back. I did ask Keith if his back was very painful but he said no, after whatever or whoever fell on his back he felt a terrible pain then no pain in that part of his anatomy any-more."

The police constables wished Lauren a speedy recovery and left. Brother Simon was not long in following, he intended to contact his parents and depart for Scotland if necessary to bring them home

Heather took a seat beside Lauren. "May I hold Hugo for just a few minutes? I love babies big and small ones, and some who are all grown up and some just as tiny as you.

Taking the offered child in her arms she shushed him just as she had all those years ago, but no, she would not remember this was not time for what might have been. It was now and if she wasn't very much mistaken Lauren was sitting wondering what to do next.

"Lauren! May call you Lauren, you have a beautiful family but you are going to need a lot of help for the next little while, does your brother live anywhere nearby? Has Charles said anything about you staying here in his house until you know your husband is on the way to recovery? Once you are back on your feet it's only about 10 minutes walk to the hospital and just up the road from here is a good school for preschoolers and a junior school, ideal for your youngsters."

Turning Heather saw a smile widening across the face of one Charles Blossom.

"What do you think? Lauren will you at least consider it," he pleaded.

Giving a great sigh of relief Lauren wiped her eyes with the back of her hand.

"Its' the best idea I have heard in ages, thank you Mrs Wilson, thank you Charles." then promptly burst into tears.

Handing the infant to Kate, Heather leaned over and taking the crying woman into her arms rocked her just as she recently rocked Christopher, but no-one knew of this it was just between her boy and herself.

Heather had time to size up the situation between her last female chick and the now returned Charles Blossom.

"By the look of you two, if I guess wedding bells are in the offing would I be right?

Before either could answer Christopher cut with, "and not before bloody time either, congratulations to you both and have you thought about a suitable time and place and last but not least, make it soon."

Kate immediately picked on the last phrase, "make it soon."

"Christopher why the hurry?, are you not telling me something and do not try and lie because I will know, which will make me worry a whole lot more."

Heather sent him a look of sympathy. "I think it must be lunch time, does anybody here like Spaghetti Bolognese? Both children nodded their heads. "Right then would you two like to watch me make the sauce, it's my secret recipe."

Jessica smiled at Heather, "yes please I would like to watch then I can make some when my Daddy comes home, it will be a surprise for him."

Her little brother spoke up. "I am not allowed to touch things in the kitchen in case I hurt myself, Mummy said so," then added, "but she didn't I couldn't watch."

"Now then Lauren would you like to have a little rest before we eat, let me help you up. There you are, now let me hold young Hugo while we go upstairs and get you both settled; then with my small helpers I will get lunch under-way."

The house was quiet, mother and baby sleeping upstairs, the muted voices of those in the kitchen in the background, leaving Charles and Kate sitting side by side on one sofa and Christopher sitting opposite.

"I had better begin at the beginning. As you know when we were trying to sort out the mess made by Lucy's step father and her half brother and sister, we engaged John Buchanan QC to sort the legalities. He is a close friend of Aubrey as well as former colleague. When Josephine and Aubrey married, John was Aubrey's Best Man and his younger sister Sybil accompanied her brother to the wedding.

Over the ensuring months I got to know Sybil very well, more than very well, I fell head over heels in love with her." He stopped to gather his thoughts, then rubbing his hand over his face continued. "We spent nearly all our spare time together, we even had several long week-ends away, and then Sybil seemed to cool off. I couldn't understand why, I don't think I had done anything to upset her. I asked her to marry me the day Josephine's Freddie was born. I made a joke about it being a sign and hoped perhaps the next new babe would be ours, hers and mine. Then I received a letter saying she had changed her mind about us and it would be better if we saw less of each other for a while to make sure we were suited."

Leaning over he took his sister's hand as though to hang onto something solid.

"What happened?" Kate questioned softly.

"Sybil didn't say anything at the time, just last summer she told me, said she had changed her mind about being my wife. When I pressed her for answer all she would say was it was her, it was never her intention to have children, not mine, not anybodies."

"She does not like children!" Charles let out a huff of breath as he parroted Christopher's words, "what is not to like about them, we all know they can be a pain in the." after a slight hesitation, "backside at times, but then so can some adults, what's her problem?"

"Later." Christopher continued, ignoring Charles interruption, "on my or rather our last visit to Josephine and Aubrey, Sybil made quite a scene when Freddie, who was just beginning to walk, toddled over to her and handed her his biscuit. As he handed it to her he toppled over but instead of falling he grabbed a hold of her skirt. Sybil was furious but instead of moving out of the little boy's way she slapped his tiny hand, not a gentle tap but a very hard slap. Freddie didn't cry he just sat with look of surprise on his little face he had never been slapped before. She glared at me when I picked him up and giving me a non to gentle push told me to take the revolting child away. Freddie started to cry. Miriam Khan appeared from nowhere to rescue Freddie and calm him down. If you think that was bad worse was to follow. Sybil really lost her cool, she berated the nanny for her lack of control and suggested until the child learned some manners it would be better if she kept him in the nursery while his parents had guests staying with them.

Miriam waited until Sybil had run out of steam before she answered, and I must say with a quiet dignity which surprised me. "

"Miss Buchannan, the Page children are both well behaved and normal babies. Freddie in his own baby way was extending to you the hand of friendship. Unfortunately you chose to either ignore this or perhaps you don't understand the way of children. If the latter is the case I would humbly suggest you take a course in child care before embarking into motherhood." Turning towards me she apologised for speaking out of turn to my guest.

"Of course when Josephine returned from morning surgery and Aubrey a little later Sybil was her usual charming self."

I did not prolong our visit and as soon as politely possible I drove back to London. I was astonished, upset and at a complete loss to understand the woman sitting next to me who I thought I knew. I drove her straight to her home; she still lives with her brother in a very upmarket house in Muswell Hill. As I drew up outside her home she asked was I coming in and if I would care to stay the night. Kate all I wanted to do was to get as far from her as possible. That is why I was allegedly going to stay with the Buchanan's for Christmas. The real reason I was going, was to explain to John Buchanan I was not going to marry his sister and if necessary explain why. I have telephoned John early this morning explaining my New Year plans have changed. I have to return to London something has come up which needs my immediate attention. Heather suggested I remain at Pipers Gate then go back to London on the 2nd January But I must go to Church House no later than the 30th I promised my sister I would be there so I must."

"Christopher, have you told Aubrey about this, perhaps he can throw some light on Sybil's behaviour but in the meantime darling brother of mine I think it's time to eat."

CHAPTER 18

It was a little before five o' clock when Christopher and Heather finally took their leave of the residents at 5 Sycamore Road with a promise to keep in touch if they needed anything or help from the McKenzie household.

To the sound of soft background music Heather was going over in her mind all of what Christopher had confided in her the night before. How could a woman act towards a small child with such abhorrence? Why Freddie was still a baby not yet two years old, "I reckon my Christopher is better off without her. My God if he had married her without knowing her aversion to children what a miserable life he would have had." Heather did not realise she had spoken out aloud. Taking his hand off the steering wheel he patted her hand.

"Heather, you are as right as ever. But enough of me, when you were holding baby Hugo I saw the same look on your face as when you first cuddled Cameron and Alistair, then Oliver and finally Freddie, then again later today. To me it said of a yearning from long time past. It was then I realised you never ever referred to the time before you came to Pipers Gate. I came when I was nearly five and my sisters were still babies, and you were there when we arrived. I remember standing in the hall before a Grandpa I didn't remember and all I wanted to do was go home and find my Daddy. I remember starting to cry and you lifted me up and gave me a cuddle then hushed me in your arms until I stopped. You said don't cry darling, Heather has you now. I won't allow anything to frighten you I will always be here if you need me."

"Christopher I remember every single thing that happened that day and will do until the day I die. Your Grandpa saved my life, and when I was feeling a little better took me into his household to help your Ma cope with her grief and manage her family.

Your Ma and me shared our grief by caring and supporting each other, she with her five children and me without mine."

As Heather drew a shuddering breath she continued her story.

"I was married on my nineteenth birthday to a lovely young man called John Joseph Wilson. We had been childhood sweethearts. It was a glorious summer day, blue sky and warm. We even had a small house, two up and two down with a kitchen at the back. My goodness we were so happy and on our first anniversary we found out we were having a baby. In due course we became the besotted parents of the most beautiful baby boy that had ever been born. He was called Jonathan Joseph almost the same as his daddy.

When Jonathan was almost three he walked and talked and was his Daddy's little shadow that is until;" for a moments Heather stopped her narrative to blow her nose before continuing. "Until one morning John woke up with a very sore throat. I tried to get him to see a doctor but he said it was most likely the start of a cold, it would be better in a couple of days. But it didn't, two days later Jonathan seemed to be out of sorts and wouldn't eat anything and seemed to have problems swallowing even water. By this time nearly half the village had more or less the same symptoms. In a short space of time it was confirmed the sore throat was in fact Diphtheria, and both my beautiful boys died. My baby on the 1st of March, and my Husband, on the 3rd of March.

Dr Drummond left me some sleeping tablets to help me rest before the funeral. Jonathan was buried with his Daddy, both my boys together. The day before the funeral I took all the sleeping pills in one go, I had nothing left to live for and I wanted to go with both my boys.

Fortunately the good Doctor called to see if I needed anything or any help to get me through the next few days. It was he who found me unconscious on the bedroom floor. It was also the day your Daddy was taken from you. So you see Christopher that is how your Ma and me held each other together. It wasn't easy, in fact sometimes I wondered why God took my only family and left me out.

It wasn't fair but I learned to take one day at a time. When your Ma cried I tried to comfort her. For the most part I often cried along with her and her with me. So over the years we have been each other's salvation. I was the lucky one; she was so generous she shared her precious children with me. I grew to love each and every one of you as though you were my own."

"I know you loved us all and we all love you back. It makes my problems look insignificant in comparison." Christopher whispered as he cried for what might have been and now what was.

"Dry your eyes Christopher, everyone's hurt is personal to them, but I promise you my boy, the right lady will come into your life and maybe sooner than you think.

So we had better put us a smiley face on because we are just about home."

CHAPTER 19

The Mini Bus deposited Daniels happy little band about one hour before Heather and Christopher arrived home. The small children had all fallen asleep on the return journey which meant they wanted to tell their Uncle Christopher all about what they had seen and done. Alistair and Cameron had the most to say, especially about the real animals in the church.

"Do you know that some cats and dogs can talk to each other," Cameron informed his uncle, "and so can rabbits and I think Nanny Goats too," Alistair piped, "I know cos' I was stroking a little Rabbit with one hand and I held the ear of the baby goat and she bleated at the Rabbit."

Christopher was aware of another little hand tugging at his leg, bending down he swung Oliver up asking him what he had liked the best. Putting his hands into Christopher's hair Oliver turned his uncle's head until they were almost nose to nose. "I see'd a Pussy-Cat who said meow to me and I see'd my Daddy, who held me up to see." here the little boy, faltered looking across the room to where his parent was in earnest conversation with his uncle Sebastian called, "Daddy what did we see?" "Excuse me Sebastian I think it will be better if we continue this conversation when the children are in bed." went over to enquire of his son what it was he wished to know. With a little prompting from his father Oliver was able to finish his conversation with his Uncle Christopher.

Then it was time for nursery supper leaving the grownups not involved in this particular ritual to relax a little before preparing for dinner.

Elizabeth drew her youngest son down beside her.

"Tell me about your day, did you find out anything further about Charles' brother's condition and how are mother and new baby?"

"In answer to your first question, not a lot, the Neuro people are still doing tests. When we arrived a couple of Police officers were with Lauren, Keith's wife." Elizabeth immediately pounced on the 'we.'

"Did you take Sybil with you?"

For the minute Christopher looked blank. ."Whatever makes you think I took Sybil Buchanan, she and her brother are not due to arrive at Church House until December 30th. No, Heather and I went together, she to see Kate and of course the new baby and me as you know to suss out the situation. But it was Heather who sorted out the problems to everybody's satisfaction."

He flashed his mother a grin, "You should have been there, Heather was giving Hugo Charles a cuddle while talking to Lauren who started to cry, and before you could blink she thrust the infant into Kate's arms so she could to attend to Lauren. At first Kate just held the babe as though not knowing quite what to do with him, then the expression on her face changed as she put her arms around him and tucked him to her. Ma it was heartbreaking to see her. She was present when her twin and her two elder brothers married. She came from the U.S of A as soon as she heard Sebastian and Christina's babies were born and she came ahead of the births for both Oliver and Freddie. It made me want to thump Jamie Tallington for making my little sister miss out on what is by right her birthright."

Elizabeth squeezed her son's arm, "don't worry I think Kate will have her own babies soon enough. From what Heather said when she spoke to me, was it only yesterday? She that is Kate and Charles Blossom will be tying the knot sooner than later."

"Well if the second Professor to join this family has anything to do with the arrangements it will be no later than the 31st January 1999."

"My goodness Christopher, that's only 35 days away."

"I shouldn't let a little thing like that worry you Ma, get your husband to organise it, he did yours in 27 days this time he has an extra 7 days to play with."

Mr Benson hovered in the upper hall waiting for Sebastian to leave his sons' bedroom before going to his own to change for dinner. After what seemed an age Sebastian left closing the door very quietly, the last thing he wanted was either of the children to request just one more story. He really must remember to write down the ones he had already told them. Cameron liked to be told about his daddy when he was a little boy, whilst Alistair would ask, "tell us about when you fell off the swing and hurt your arm. Did it hurt a lot and did your mummy kiss it better?" Alistair liked all the gory details.

"Good Evening Mr Sebastian, may I have a word, it is important."

"Good evening Mr Benson of course." but instead of replying Mr Benson handed him the written message from Jim Harris.

The butler left Sebastian to read the message in private.

Quickly scanning the note he pondered for a moment or two as though undecided what to do next. However instead of returning to his room he slipped down to Grandpa's study. Closing the door behind him he then dialled a direct line to Jim Harris where he had Jim tell him in detail as much as he could remember of Dr and Mrs Walsh.

"Jim what was the first thing you saw when they arrived? Which bell did they ring?"

"I'll take the second question first; they rang the company bell, McKenzie S.I. Ltd which you know comes straight to me when there is no one else in residence. It was the woman who spoke first she asked for Patrick McKenzie neither Mr Patrick McKenzie nor the company name. She spoke with an Irish accent, not Ulster more of a softer southern sound.

Then the man spoke and I heard him say, let me talk to him I'm not sure whether he meant Patrick or me. After I explained the family were away until the 4th of January she asked if she might leave a message. It was important as she was Aunt to Patrick McKenzie's wife. It was at this point I decided to let them inside. It was freezing cold out in the street and they would soon start drawing attention to themselves if they insisted on leaving Mrs Lucy a message on the entrance phone.

When they came in I didn't particularly like what I saw. The man introduced himself as Dr Peter Walsh and his wife as Mrs Rosalie Walsh sister to one Aidan Forsythe, who is Mrs Lucy's father. But she didn't call her niece Lucy or Lucinda she called her Lindsay. I asked them to write down what they wanted and I would pass their message on.

As I was talking to them I noticed the Doctor seemed to have his eyes all over the place. I knew that look Mr Sebastian, I done the same myself before I came to work for the McKenzie family. Then his wife asked did Lindsay and Patrick live on the premises, and did anybody else live here and who exactly was I and did I regularly stay here or just when the family were away.

I reckon this pair is trouble with a capital T; I didn't answer any of their questions I just waited to see what happened next. When they realised I was not going to answer their questions Mrs Walsh said not to worry they would come again when you returned to London, or perhaps they may have time to go to Suffolk before the New Year. As they were leaving I heard her husband say "Why did you have to open your mouth and mention Suffolk, that fellow on the door will let them know about our visit before we are out of the street."

"Jim, leave it with me I think one of us will be returning to London by 30th December latest, I'm not quite sure who it will be but will keep you posted. In the meantime have a word with the desk sergeant at the Marylebone Police station and ask if he can arrange a regular drive round, just over the holiday period, no need to go into details."

"Dam and Blast," Sebastian muttered under his breath as he strode through to the small sitting room hoping to find his brother-in-law Aubrey, but he was out of luck. Christopher was there with Fiona and Michael who were relating their adventure of the day.

Christopher was mildly surprised Michael Shaw had joined in with such enthusiasm but he did Michael an injustice. Michael lost no time in retelling of the little ones antics especially Freddie who desperately tried to keep up with his older brother and cousins.

"He is trying so hard to talk, yes we all know he can say many words singularly and in some cases string two or three together to make a coherent small sentence, but today he got a tad frustrated especially when he wanted one of his parents attention to some detail he had seen." Turning to his sister went on to say, "you seemed to get along great with Oliver and Sebastian's pair. You should have seen her with the boys, showing them how to hold a baby rabbit without squeezing it to death." Michael laughed at his sister's expression."Don't you dare try to tell me you didn't enjoy your day out Fiona Shaw, you were wrapped up in everything the guide told us about Lavenham Church, and the Market Square simply blew you away."

"Sorry to but in, has Aubrey come down yet?

A voice spoke from behind him. "I believe he is waiting until Josephine give her boys one last bedtime kiss, they won't be more than a few minutes."

"Patrick, Sebastian swung round and taking his younger brother by the arm steered him out of the doorway and towards Grandpa's study.

Closing the door behind him Sebastian gave Patrick the note from Jim Harris.

Taking his time before commenting on the contents of the note Patrick seemed to weigh up his words very carefully before replying.

"Sebastian will you keep this to yourself for a little while longer, I have a very good reason for asking and in a little while you will understand. I do not want anything to spoil my Lucy's time here. We have something to tell you or rather the family but more of that later. Perhaps we can arrange a meeting in the morning. The four of us, this could turn into a nasty situation for all of us."

CHAPTER 20

The following morning the inhabitants of Pipers Gate awoke to a white world. During the night Mr Jack Frost had paid a visit to parts of East Anglia which included Brackonfield. The garden looked a veritable fairy land.

Michael held Freddie up to the window showing the infant the spider webs glistening in the early sunshine.

"Look see how it sparkles." taking the baby hand in his Michael pointed the small finger towards the tree immediately outside the window. "Oh! Look baby, it's a Robin Red Breast." and sure enough the little bird depicted on so many Christmas cards alighted on the tree so close Michael felt as though he could reach out and touch it.

Aubrey watched the young man holding the little boy and wondered if some time in the near future he would realise his calling was to follow Josephine and perhaps specialize in Paediatrics. Time would tell, turning towards the dining room Aubrey met up with all three brothers-in-law hovering just inside the door.

"I have arranged to have sole use of Grandpa's study from ten o'clock onwards, Michael and Fiona are going to help organise a play group with the mums."

Sebastian smiled as he said this, it was obvious he would have much rather have spent time with his children. For him their babyhood would not last much longer. Now they had reached their third birthday their father knew only too well how time seemed to fly by.

But another surprise was on the cards for the meeting, one which none of the four male adults had envisaged. It seemed as though the end of year 1998 may well have some surprises in store.

After breakfast, with the children and their mothers gainfully employed the four men met as arranged.

It was Patrick who spoke first. "Before we start discussing the latest turn of events I have not told Lucy anything about the visit of Rosalie Walsh and her husband. I want to see where this going first."

Turning to Aubrey, Patrick continued; "this must have come as a terrible shock to you, after all these years to turn up on the doorstep."

Aubrey looked at the three McKenzie men, their faces serious waiting for his reply.

Taking his time to make sure they could not misunderstand one word of what he was about to say addressed all three.

"Sebastian, Patrick, Christopher. What I felt for Rosalie Forsythe all those years ago is totally and irrevocably long gone. The first time I met your sister Josephine I knew she was going to mean something very special to me and when we came back to 27 Bedford Square that magical night 19th December at the end of 1994 I knew I wanted to marry her, and I want you all to remember the day I promised to Have and to Hold From This Day Forward, to love, cherish and protect her, I meant those vows. I loved Josephine then and if it is possible I love her more than ever now. So no, Rosalie poses no threat to my marriage."

The three men watching Aubrey had the grace to look shamefaced in questioning the man who had won their sister's heart.

Sebastian cleared his throat then suggested they get on with what the original reason for the meeting in first place.

"This can be broken down into three parts.

1. Where have Dr and Mrs Walsh been before coming to London?
2. Why did they come to the house when a telephone call would have established who was or in this case not at 27 Bedford Square?

3. What do they really want?

It's my belief they or rather Rosalie has been in touch with her brother in America."

"Or perhaps been to the States and visited him." interrupted Christopher.

"Whatever, I find it strange they have left it so long in trying to see Lucy, we have been married for almost four years, well three years and ten months." Patrick amended with a grin, "seems just like yesterday."

"The important question is; how do we to deal with this intrusion?" Sebastian looking round the table directed his question to Aubrey.

"I think you should arrange a meeting by yourself Sebastian as the head of the family. Leaving them in no doubt you will decide what is best for everybody in and connected to the family McKenzie. As for their motive for seeking out Patrick and Lucy, it could be a genuine desire to meet her niece but for some reason I cannot explain I think there is a great deal more to it than just that."

"Right you are all agreed I will telephone Jim Harris with instructions to take a telephone number where we can contact them and arrange a meeting at No 27 after the 4th of January." confirmed Sebastian.

However, as the four occupants of Grandpa's study made ready to leave there was a knock on the door. "We're coming." called Patrick but before they could move out Elizabeth came in followed by Michael and Fiona Shaw.

"May we come in? Elizabeth gave her eldest son an apologetic smile but Michael and Fiona wish to have a private word with you all together, and I thought this would be an ideal opportunity." She ushered the brother and sister into the room. By this time it was more than a little crowded with seven adults.

It was Michael who spoke first. "Sebastian we want to do something and I hope you will agree." Taking a breath he started again. "Sebastian,

Fiona and I would very much like to change our surname by deed pole. We want to take your name, McKenzie that is if you will permit us to.

You and your family have taken us in, given us a home but most of all, cared for us and made us part of your family, the McKenzie family and we would very much like to become McKenzie's to."

This was the last thing any of the men present had expected.

It was Patrick who spoke first. "Are you absolutely sure, this is something you both want? For all time, it's not something just for Christmas."

"Certainly not," retorted Michael. " We wrote to Dad and he wasn't very pleased about it but as he rightly said, he will have to change his name when he comes out of prison especially as they haven't caught." for an instance his voice broke before he continued ,"the people who murdered our mother."

Sebastian moved to the young man's side, placing an arm about his shoulders he drew him to his side.

"I have no objection to a change of name for you both," turning towards the others waited for their response.

"No problem for me." said Christopher, "nor me," responded Patrick with lopsided grin.

"What's wrong with Page," Aubrey wanted to know.

"Nothing replied Fiona but we want to be McKenzie's."

"Well that settled," said Elizabeth with a sigh of relief," shall we go through its coffee time and I have a suspicion Heather has arranged a surprise for us all."

As they all headed for the small sitting room Sebastian informed the young Shaw's of his intention to return to London on 4th of January.

"If you two come with us until your vacation is over we can start the ball rolling re the change of name."

Heather was just about to send Mr Benson to see what was keeping the occupants of Grandpa's study with a reminder her special hot chocolate muffins are best eaten hot with smile on the side, to let him know there were plenty for the staff to have with their mid-morning break.

During a lull in the conversation Patrick drew Lucy to one side.

"How would you like to go out for the day tomorrow, just you and me?"

"Before taking a sip of her coffee Lucy thought for a moment, "yes it will be lovely just the two of us. Please don't get me wrong love but it's been so hectic these past few days. Time out as I said just you and me."

"Next, where would you like to go?"

"Oh no Patrick, this is your call, you know I will be happy to go anywhere so long as it with you."

"So Mrs Patrick McKenzie you're on, it's to be a surprise." Slipping an arm round her shoulders Patrick whispered, "you know I had no idea what fun is it being a husband."

"What are you two giggling about." demand a voice from the door

"Oh my good lord, Great Aunt Grace."

"No Patrick, I am not your good lord, but as you have noted, your Great Aunt, and you have not answered my question."

Lucy looked on in amazement, her husband former professional soldier, a former part of one the world famous fighting group known as The Para's, now a partner of the prestigious firm McKenzie S.I Ltd was shuffling his feet.

"Well are you going to tell me or is it something you would rather keep to yourself."

Lucy squeezed his hand offering him her silent support. "I was just telling my wife Lucy how much fun it is being a Husband."

Grace Drummond all six feet of her swooped across the room and enfolded her great nephew in an exuberant embrace. Stepping back so as to allow Patrick to breath she smiled at the man she was holding. "You are a good man Patrick and very like your father, he would have been so very proud of you."

Patrick leaned forward and kissed his great Aunt and whispered very softly, "I loved him too, very much and thank you, I also love you, lots."

"Well, now we are all here has anybody seen Kate since I sent her to rescue Professor Blossom?

Rather than saying who had or in some cases have not, those who had, simply held up their hands.

Pointing a finger at Christopher she requested he brought his great Aunt up to date.

When he had finished his narrative Great Aunt Grace asked the all important question.

"Where is Kate now?"

"Still in Cambridge, but she is going to live with Charles in Keith Blossom's house in Bedfordshire, in a place called Ampthill, a small market town to the south west of Bedford. They that is, Kate and Charles are getting married before 31st January 1999, Charles doesn't believe in long engagements." Christopher was hastening to add.

Turning back to her niece Grace said gently, "by my reckoning she seems to have taken a leaf out of your book Elizabeth, you and

Daniel gave us just about 27 day, at least your daughter has given you another seven."

The rest of the morning was spent on catching up with the news with exception of the advent of one Doctor and Mrs Walsh. This was something to be discussed after the male McKenzie's returned to London. Aubrey would arrange a date and time to join them once he returned to his own home.

CHAPTER 21

The next morning was still as beautiful as the day before. As Patrick drove through the Suffolk lanes, the hedgerows sparkled like miles of Christmas decorations. The wide open sky was an astonishing duck egg blue. The kind of sky which is associated with frosty winter days.

Lucy sat back and gave a contented little sigh. She hadn't asked where they were going, she knew Patrick well enough to know wherever they ended up it would be somewhere they could both enjoy, either the scenery or perhaps a National Trust Property, whatever, she was happy to be with her beloved Patrick.

As though he could guess what she was thinking Patrick placed his hand on her knee, giving it a little squeeze at the same time saying; "Happy love, we are going to the sea-side, Felixstowe for a walk along the prom, then lunch in that lovely old fashioned restaurant overlooking the sea front. How does that appeal to you?"

"Just what the doctor ordered. It seems such a long time since we visited Felixstowe."

She settled back in her seat to enjoy the day.

Back at Pipers Gate Daniel was just about to bang the gong for lunch (Mr Benson allowed Daniel this dubious honour because Daniel had confessed he enjoyed making a very loud sound without having to apologise) when there was a resounding bang on the front door which was repeated at least twice before anybody got to the door in time to open it. Daniel had relinquished the gong in order to investigate who was demanding entry at this time of day. He couldn't remember if anyone was invited to lunch, but then they hadn't anticipated Elizabeth's Aunt Grace the day before, and she had stayed right through to almost bedtime.

Mr Benson opened the door, where before him stood two strangers or rather strangers to him, but after Mr Jim Harris' description of these two it was obvious Dr and Mrs Walsh had found their way to Pipers Gate.

It was Mrs Walsh who spoke first. "We, that is I, have come to see my niece Mrs Patrick McKenzie. I believe she is staying here over the holiday." As she was speaking she stepped inside the hall.

"If you will please wait in here I will see if Mr McKenzie is at home." Mr Benson enjoyed the look of surprise on the face of Mrs Walsh as he ushered them into a pleasant if small room to the left of the front door.

Crossing the hall he entered the main dining-room where Sebastian was in the process of helping himself to a large portion of Heather's special steak and ale pie. Bending down so as to keep his brief conversation private he told him he had some unexpected callers in the morning room.

For the moment Sebastian looked blank, and then he remembered, the morning room was a joke, that was where his mother had put anyone who needed what she called a five minute time out to cool off. If that didn't work she hauled them in Grandpa's study without further argument for a serious talk. It nearly always worked, well at least 98% of the time.

"Who is it and what do they want?"

"I believe it is Dr and Mrs Walsh Sir."

Sebastian raised his eyebrows, it was obvious their very proper butler didn't like the visitors hence the "Sir."

As Mr Benson opened the door he had made sure that the Doctor and his wife heard him address Mr Sebastian as Sir.

Advancing into the room Sebastian said; "Sebastian McKenzie what can I do to help you?" Indicating a couple chairs, he invited his unexpected visitors to sit down.

The Walsh's sat, for a moment no one spoke. Sebastian remained silent, they wanted something then they would have to ask. It was the oldest trick in the book, the silence was deafening, but Sebastian uttered not a word.

Finally it was Mrs Walsh who spoke first, "I have come a long way to see my niece, it's been a long time since I have seen little Lindsay and I promised my brother I would go and make sure she is well and happy." As she finished speaking Rosalie took out a tissue and blotted her eyes.

Sebastian had been in the London Metropolitan Police for quite a number of years before starting his own business but he had not lost his edge or nose or whatever you care to call it. He knew when something was not quite kosher and from where he was sitting this lady just did not ring true.

"I'm sorry you have had a wasted journey, Patrick and his wife are away at present. I understand you called at No 27 Bedford Square a couple of days ago. If you care to leave your telephone number we will contact you upon our return to London. We expect to be there by the 4th of January. Or if you prefer, leave your details where you are staying, I will arrange for one of us to call on you."

Looking at his watch Sebastian suggested they visit the local pub. "The Lion and the Snake do an excellent lunch until about 2.30pm."

His uninvited guests stood up, handing Sebastian his card Dr Walsh had scribbled the address of their hotel and telephone number.

As Sebastian was ushering them towards the front door Michael came into the hall looking for him.

"There you are Sebastian, Aunt Elizabeth asked me to find you," and was about to say and tell you your lunch is getting cold, when he caught sight of the couple going through the front door.

"We will look forward to meeting you and little Lindsay in the New Year," called Rosalie.

Sebastian closed the door behind them and turning saw Michael standing as though turned to stone.

"Michael! Whatever is the matter?" Instead of answering the young man started to shake at the same time reaching out to hold onto Sebastian as though he was a lifeline.

Mr Benson had been hovering in the hall came to Sebastian's aide.

"Help me get him into the little sitting room." This was accomplished with a minimum of fuss.

Mr Benson handed Michael a small brandy, at the same time assuring Sebastian a little for medicinal purposes wouldn't hurt.

When Sebastian was satisfied Michael was recovering he asked Mr Benson to fetch Mr Aubrey when the said gentleman had finished his lunch.

After the departure of the butler Michael spoke.

"That was her, it was her voice I heard the night my mother was killed." Turning to the man he regarded as his Guardian continued, you know when we talked after Lucy and Patrick's wedding, I told you on the dreadful night I heard voices then a funny sound followed by a thud. At the time I didn't remember what kind of voice it was. But just now I recognised it; it was that woman who has just left."

"Michael can you remember if she saw either you are your sister."

"I don't think so unless she had been watching the house during the day. But somehow I don't think she would."

"Have you any idea why not?"

"Because ever since the attack on Lucy, she was Lindsay then, the police never let up on trying to find out who was responsible for the awful injuries inflicted on my sister."

"Do you mean there was a constant police presence?"

"Not all the time, but a car would come round at odd times and a foot patrol would do a walk by sometimes twice a day sometimes three times or no times at all. I think they, the police did this to keep whoever was responsible on the hop. Because whoever was responsible for Lindsay's appalling injuries would never know if or when Lindsay's memory would come back."

"Michael I want you to tell Aubrey all you know and actually remember when he comes in, but do not under any circumstances say a word to anyone else. We don't want Lucy upset. Patrick will tell her when he thinks it's the right time. Don't say a word to Fiona either. Wait until we all return to London then we will have a meeting which I hope will tie up all the loose ends once and for all.

Sebastian returned to the dining-room to find the rest were almost finished their pudding. Cameron hailed his father while at the same time lifting up his plate.

"Look Daddy, I'm all done," but after intercepting a shake of the head from his mother changed tack." Daddy, I have eaten all of my diner, and all my pudding but I left some sprouts. May I please get down?"

"Me to Daddy look." called Alistair.

Sebastian looked first at his wife then his boys, "has your Mummy finished?"

The children looked towards Christina, and noted she still had some pudding not yet eaten. "I haven't started mine and I would very much like you to stay until I have had time to hear all about what you did this morning."

This was said in a quiet tone of voice but left the little boys in no doubt their father expected them to remain seated until he was ready for all them to leave the table.

Sebastian was not being unduly stern but he wanted his children to learn from an early age that good manners and social niceties would be expected of them. Also it would give them time to digest their meal because immediately he was free he intended to indulge them in a game of McKenzie football.

This was a game played with a large soft ball with no holds barred. This usually meant Sebastian being Goalie and attacked by all the small people available, and taking into account Michael and Uncle Christopher thought they were still small boys it usually ended a tangle of arms and legs.

In the meantime Michael waylaid Aubrey and explained what had happened just as lunch was being served.

"Do you think Mrs Walsh recognised you Michael?

"No I'm sure she didn't really notice me and I don't recall seeing her near the house in Gosforth."

"I have to ask you this Michael could you have been mistaken, about the woman I mean not the voice?"

"No Aubrey, I am one hundred percent certain it was her. It wasn't just the tone of her voice it was when she said *Little Lindsay* she used that expression that night."

"Just one more question Michael, would your sister either recognise her or her voice?"

"I don't think so she has never mentioned it to me besides it was me who was downstairs listening that night and it was only later Fiona became involved." Michael shivered, recollecting that dreadful night when his mother died.

Aubrey explained to the young man what had been discussed earlier in the day.

"It has been agreed Sebastian will arrange a meeting when we have returned to our homes after the holiday. As you know we, that is the Page family and yourselves are going home to Church House tomorrow. On the 31st Lucy and Patrick are to join us as is Christopher, although in view with what has happened he may go straight back to London. Sebastian and family are staying here and return to Richmond on the 4th of January. As for Kate," here Aubrey allowed himself a slow smile, "it largely depends on Simon Young's powers of persuasion in getting his parents back to England before Hogmanay."

Michael soon to be McKenzie, turned for the door then stopped mid stride, half turning he asked in slightly sly voice. "Are we to have another wedding any time soon?"

"Have you anyone in mind." replied the older man with an equally sly smile.

"How about little bet Aubrey, are you up for it?"

"You can say I might be interested."

"How about 10 to 1 on, we have a wedding before Easter?"

"Right friend you're on; Tens it is."

"Are you two laying bets that my beautiful daughter will be married by Easter?"

Both males jumped almost a foot at the sound of Elizabeth's voice, although Aubrey was to say later his mother-in-law was exaggerating.

"Of course not, we were just commenting how all the McKenzie weddings seemed to take place just before or after Easter, "answered Michael trying to keep the laughter from his voice.

"Shall I take your bets, Michael I believe you suggested 10-1 on, and you Aubrey I think I heard you agree for and against an Easter wedding," she waited, "no takers, wise; men. Shall I let you into a secret, the wedding will be between now and the 31st January 1999. She allowed herself a little smirk as she walked away leaving them with their collective mouths open.

CHAPTER 22

Meanwhile Christopher had been busy on two very different issues, after a long telephone call made to John Buchanan QC requesting he and John had a private meeting before the 31st December at 27 Bedford Square relative to his recent breakup with Sybil. He didn't go into detail but stated he had not done so without a great deal of soul searching on his part. "I will be in London tomorrow until about three in the afternoon."

After John agreed and hung up, Christopher then put a call through on their direct line hoping to speak to Jim Harris. He was in luck it was the man himself who answered.

"What's up Christopher? I thought you would have been painting your part of the world a delicate shade of red by now, in preparation for the New Year celebrations."

"No such luck, I am returning to London on the 29th I reckon I should be with you round about ten to ten thirty providing the traffic is not too bad.

Your visitors the Walsh's turned up here just round lunch time. Sebastian was not pleased one little bit.

However, the reason I rung is to ask if you have changed the CCTV film since we left for Brackonfield? If you have please put it in a place of safety, if it's still as we left it change as soon as I ring off and lock it away. I will explain why it's important when I join you. I am having a visitor in the morning, Mr John Buchanan, on his own; Miss Buchanan will not be joining us. Tell your Mum not to worry about lunch I will take Mr Buchanan out somewhere."

"Christopher I took the CCTV film out immediately Dr and Mrs Walsh left, a new one has been inserted fresh every morning since. Just in case, we don't want any more nonsense like when some bad boys decided they would try and upset McKenzie SI Ltd. That was a night to remember, but of course you missed it being as you were out chasing up mischief in the Emerald Isle. Might I ask if the Walsh's are part of this latest ripple on the quiet waters of the firm?"

"Yes Jim I think so but in a more obscure way, I will try to bring you into the loop day after tomorrow."

Putting the phone down Christopher sat in the stillness of his Grandpa's study.

He remembered his Grandpa McKenzie, a giant of a man with his no nonsense approach to life. He loved hearing how he Grandpa Mac had found his daddy as a little baby crawling in the undergrowth on the side of the highway in North America in a place just outside Buffalo. How he had picked up the little child covered in blood and filthy dirty. The child's parents had been killed in an auto-mobile accident and no one had noticed the little boy who had been flung clear of the carnage.

How one Doctor McKenzie had taken the little one home to clean him up before calling the authorities, but of course when Mrs McKenzie, who was to become their Grandma saw the babe she put her foot down very firmly and said they were going to adopt him. Although this took a great deal more effort because the child was pure bred indigenous Native of North America, a direct descendent of the Arapaho Indian tribe.

He remembered how the two Grandpas met, one a Doctor in up-state New York in a town called Pulaski and the other a Doctor in a country area of Suffolk, but both had a very special place in Christopher McKenzie's heart. They loved him and he loved them straight back.

He sat at the same desk as his Scottish Grandpa and leaning over placed his head on his arms.

"Grandpas I need you advice, no make that help. This woman Mrs Walsh has capacity to make difficulties for Patrick's Lucy. She calls herself her Aunt, but I don't trust her. My gut feeling is she intends to hurt and disrupt several lives, Josephine's, Aubrey, who I love like a brother and then the young Shawcross', who are soon to become McKenzie's. Not unlike you Grandpa McKenzie, except this pair are not small children but young adults. If either or both of you can help, I'm not sure what I am asking is possible, but please do your best."

Christopher closed his eyes in silent prayer, and as he allowed himself to relax he sensed rather than felt a warm breath on his face while at the same time hearing a voice inside his head saying "keep the faith my boy all will be well."

He must have dozed for about an hour when he was woken by a small hand stroking the side of his face.

"Unca Christopher, are you too tired to play ball with us?" Alistair asked his little face screwed up with concern.

"You can play first if you would like to," this was a great concession on Cameron's part, he liked everything to be orderly and big Uncles where expected to take their turn like everybody else.

Scooping his twin nephews up into his arms Christopher nuzzled his face into their heads.

"Boys, I am ready for anything, who is being goalie this time?"

"Grandpa Daniel, Grandma said he can play for half an hour," then came the inevitable; "What is half an hour?"

Their uncle ever wise to this tactic replied, "I will explain later, now who is going to kick off."

After thirty minutes of no holds barred soft ball Grandpa Daniel called halt. "I think we should call this match a draw and ignoring the calls for more play informed all present tea was being served in the small dining room with sandwiches, cakes and jelly with ice-cream.

"It is amazing how much food this lot can put away after time outside in the fresh air;" Heather remarked to Mr Benson.

"Mrs Wilson, not only the fresh air, it's the activities, with nearly all the male members of the family which makes the difference. Have you noticed how even the youngest, young Oliver tries to keep up; he is an amazing little boy."

"I quite agree he takes after his mother in many respects and much like his Aunty Kate. She would not let anything stop her once she had set her sights on what she wanted to do."

"You are very fond of them Mrs Wilson, it must have been hard when they started leaving the nest."

"Yes Mr Benson it was at first, but you know, they always came back either here or Bedford Square, my." Heather stopped to blow her nose, "enough of all our yesterdays it's time for round up and teatime."

Mr Benson looked after Heather's retreating figure, she should have had some of her own, looking after somebody else's was a sad substitute for your own children. He straightened his shoulders and headed down the hall to his domain, work dulled the pain, but it doesn't go away said a small still voice in his head.

CHAPTER 23

While all the excitement was taking place at Pipers Gate, a solitary figure was aimlessly walking round the village of Brackonfield. Without any particular destination in mind the walker stopped outside the parish church.

It was just past four pm on a cold winter's afternoon, and with a sigh which seemed to come from the very bottom of his soul turned and entered the churchyard through the Lynch Gate.

Walking towards the church doors he looked down at the headstones lining the path as though to refresh his memory. Of course he knew the names on every grave, they where his family stretching as far back as 1703. "I wonder if any of you made such a hash of things as me. I had within my grasp one of the most wonderful gifts ever bestowed on man and I not only threw it away but managed to trample on it first."

Slipping inside the church to find it was too late to retreat without causing a disturbance he slid into a pew near the back. Evensong had just started, the inside of the church was partially lit, and the giant Christmas tree glowed with dozens of pretty tree lights. As the service proceeded the sense of timeless tranquillity seemed to wash over him.

Falling to his knees he bowed his head and prayed for forgiveness and the strength to put the past behind him. He didn't expect the former but prayed for peace of mind.

"Please God make the pain go away." He didn't realise he had spoken out allowed

Fortunately not one of the few worshippers turned to see who had spoken, but someone had heard the softly spoken words. Continuing with the service the vicar hoped the late comer would remain seated until after the small congregation left.

The back of the church was in semi darkness, and the man on his knees was unaware the service was now over. It wasn't until a hand touched his arm and a quiet voice asked the all important question.

"Mr Tallington, are you unwell?" Jamie Tallington came back from the pit his dark thoughts had taken him. He looked blank for a minute or two, before realizing the vicar was standing by his side asking if she could help.

Shaking his head he made to rise from his knees in preparation to leave.

"Its' alright Vicar just having a bad day, I had some news I knew was on the cards, but had hoped would not happen."

"Are you or a member of your family ill?"

"No the family are all well, as for me how you deal with lost dreams, broken promises, knowing there is no one to blame but myself." His voice broke as he finished. Afraid he was going to cry he stumbled to his feet, but the same gentle hand pressed him down onto the seat.

"Would you care to come to tea, my son will have returned from his walk with my housekeeper and will be ready for his. We always have toasted crumpets after evensong in the winter it bridges the gap between lunch and supper."

She waited, would this man who looked as though whatever he had or had not done was at the end of his tether.

Jamie just nodded. "Yes please I would like that."

"Right then if you come down to the front with me, I want to wish my Church Warden goodnight; we can then leave by the side door it's just a few steps to home."

Jamie Tallington was to remember those words, *"its' just a few steps to home."* in a different place in a time yet to come, but with same meaning, *Hope*.

Summoning up a semblance of a smile Jamie rose from his seat and followed the Vicar as suggested.

Entering the front door the vicar indicated the row of coat hooks.

"Hang your coat and scarf here, we have fixed the coat hooks above the radiator, this keeps the coats and things warm ready for braving the wind and cold outside. Come this way Mr Tallington."

As Laura Featherstone spoke she opened a door to her left.

The room looked warm and inviting, sprawled on the floor in front of a roaring fire was a young boy reading. Jamie couldn't make out what it was holding the child's attention from where he stood but whatever it was, the boy was totally absorbed and paid no attention to the arrival of a stranger in their mist.

"Edward, I see you have the tea things organised, thank you, but would you mind taking your head out of whatever you are reading and say hello to Mr Tallington."

Turning his head towards Jamie responded with a polite "Hello, have you come to join us for tea, we are having toasted crumpets and a super Victoria Sponge with lashing of fresh cream and strawberry jam. Mummy made it this morning after the late morning service. While I was waiting for her to finish, I got all the ingredients out ready for the cake I mean, we bought the crumpets." he ended this statement with a chuckle.

Getting up from the floor Edward put his hand out to steady himself then turning towards the voice in the doorway repeated "are you staying to tea?"

"Yes please it's a long time since I had crumpets toasted in front of a real fire." replied Jamie.

"Good, would you like to come and sit here, we don't sit at the table for a winter day teatime." Edward indicated a chair near to the fire and waiting until Jamie was seated, explained he couldn't see him but he could feel him.

"I lost my eyes when I was a little boy, no, not lost them as mislaid, but couldn't see any-more.

We were in an accident, my Daddy went to heaven, and left us, Mummy with a gammy leg, and me with what is called impaired vision." These facts were told in such a matter of fact way as to prevent any hint of self pity.

Jamie waited he wasn't sure what to say in response, what could he say to a youngster who couldn't see him. A well of pity surged up in him from nowhere; this woman and her son were getting on with their lives despite the dreadful circumstances they had had to contend with, while he the great Jamie Tallington was whinging about Kate McKenzie marrying someone other than himself.

He had to get out of here; he had no business burdening this woman with his self induced pain.

As though sensing Jamie's intention to leave before Jamie was aware of it himself Edward laid his hand on the arm of the silent man. "Do sit down Mr Tallington, Mummy will be here in just a tick then we'll have tea. It's nice to have company, we don't get many visitors. Oh dear, I mean we have lots of people come to see the Vicar, but not many just to see us."

"Of course I'll stay as I said it's a long time since I had real toasted crumpets and who can resist them. I also happen to be rather partial to Victoria Sponge Cake."

At this last remark Laura returned and smiling at her guest said."OK I think we will ask Mr Tallington if he will do the honours and start toasting while I pour the tea and you Edward hand out the plates and don't forget the napkins otherwise we will end up covered in hot butter."

He son laughed."You mean you will, I just cannot understand how you make such a mess and yet me, who is blind can manage to eat a hot toasted crumpet covered in butter without getting it all down my front."

"Because you cheat, you horrid little boy." retorted his mother, "you don't eat it flat but fold the edges up like a saucer so all the butter runs round into the centre."

"Yummy you should try it sometime." returned her son laughing his head off.

"Mr Tallington, I will show you how to do it if you like, it's ever so easy once you get the knack of it."

Jamie watched as the banter flew between mother and son. He himself, part of a large family was well used to family chitchat and banter between his parents and his brothers and sisters, but this was something special between two people who appeared to be survivors.

After tea Jamie was preparing to take his leave when Edward asked if he would stay on for a game of Triominoes.

"Triominoes, what are they? I've played Dominoes, are they the same?"

"No, not quite the same, but nearly," responded Edward with a laugh in his voice.

"Mummy is good in fact very good. Although anyone can play providing you can count."

Casting a glance in his mother's direction asked, "will you explain the rules to Mr Tallington, I'm sure he will grasp the general idea very quickly."

"Before we start will you do something for me, will you drop the Mr Tallington and call me Jamie, otherwise I will be obliged to call you Master Edward and address your mother Vicar."

At this last remark Edward almost rolled about laughing and was joined by his mother laughing just as hard.

"Sorry did I say something funny?" Jamie knew he was sounding affronted but he really couldn't remember saying anything to cause such hilarity.

"Oh Jamie you must excuse us, we are not laughing at you, it was just the bit about addressing me as "Vicar." exclaimed Laura wiping her eyes. "It's a standing joke in the family. When I had my first parish about seven years ago we had a very formal church warden, a good man but more than a little pompous, and whenever he had any kind of conversation with me he always ended every sentence with the word Vicar, pronouncing VICAR in individual capital letters. So we will call you Jamie if you will call us by our Christian names. As you know my son is Edward and I'm Laura. Now that's settled shall we start otherwise we will be here until bedtime."

After a hilarious hour of what could be best described as a complete shambles, the two adults and one child decided they would call it a draw.

Jamie looked at his watch and was pleasantly surprised, the time had passed so quickly but it was now time to go. Turning to Edward he took the youngster's hand saying, "Edward it is a long time since I have had so much fun, it has been a pleasure talking to you. Perhaps your mother will allow me to have a return match once I have brushed up on my maths."

"Jamie I'm sure this can be arranged but you are welcome to drop by any time you want to talk, before you leave I will give you my telephone number." replied Laura, "if you will excuse me I will get you my card."

Leaving Edward and their guest Laura went into her study to get her telephone number with details when she was available, she realised she and Jamie Tallington hadn't had the opportunity to talk of what appeared to be hurting him. Perhaps next time and suddenly realised she hoped there would be a next time. Silly lady, he is a man with issues and you are just a pair of ears willing to listen. Ah well that is part of the job so do not get involved on a personal basis.

Seeing Jamie to the door they both waved him off, each hoping he would keep his promise to visit again, although each with a different agenda.

CHAPTER 24

Patrick and Lucy blissfully unaware of the various dramatic happenings back at Brackonfield; had arrived at Felixstowe in time to enjoy a leisurely lunch. The restaurant was a family favourite with the McKenzie family.

"When we were little kids, and some of us not so little, we used to come down here every summer for two weeks holiday. The sun seemed to shine all the time. I cannot remember it raining. Now that is interesting."

"Why?

"Because Lucy, I am sure it must have rained sometime, but it just seems to me if it did, we didn't notice."

"Probably because you were all too busy doing what boys of a certain age did in those far of days." replied his wife with a grin.

"Well I will have you know young lady I didn't ogle the girls, I don't think I looked at girls that way until you came along."

"Patrick McKenzie, are you trying to have me believe you didn't look at girls until you reached the ripe old age of thirty four."

Lucy stopped dead in the middle of the promenade and turning to face her husband of three years and ten months, leaned towards him and kissed lightly on the mouth. "Patrick you nearly had me believing you but I'm pleased you waited for me, sunshine of my smile. Now then lover boy let us step out smartly before we have to return to the festivities at Pipers Gate." Linking her arm through Patrick's, they turned towards the promenade once again to complete their walk.

Driving home in the December twilight they spoke of their future plans for 1999.

"It is going to be all change again, another new beginning Patrick."

"You mean another arrival." replied her husband with a chuckle and I have a sneaking feeling there will be more than one."

"What do you mean more than one, surely you cannot be sure at this early stage" responded Lucy. Patrick placed his hand lightly on his wife's thigh.

"No sweetheart I know I have the gift of intuition but not second sight. Although I have to admit it would certainly make McKenzie history to produce two sets of twins."

"Then it would probably set Aubrey and Josephine off again trying to keep up." laughed Lucy. "Back to your first remark love, apart from us who did you have in mind?"

"Well just between us I have a suspicion Christina and Sebastian are going to be proud parents again. I overheard Sebastian asking his Mrs if she was feeling OK on Christmas morning."

"And what did you overhear her say?"

"Nothing because she was in their bedroom and he was just about to go down stairs so I missed her reply."

"So my darling delightful husband when do we tell the family?"

Giving her thigh a slight squeeze Patrick thought a minute the "how about this evening after supper but promise me you won't cry I cannot bear to see you upset."

"Patrick there is nothing to cry about, having a baby, especially a McKenzie baby it's a very joyful occasion. You know I only wish I had had a camera with me when the doctor confirmed I was pregnant. The emotions crossing your face were truly amazing. Joy, Love, excitement, apprehension, and back to tenderness all directed at me and our baby just starting to grow inside me."

"What a lovely moment just you and me together sharing in the most exciting news in the world." replied Patrick his voice choking a little.

"Come on sweetheart let's get home and give the family our good tidings."

They arrive home just after six o'clock in the midst of a family game of charades.

"Unca Patrick, Aunty Lucy, come and play. Grandpa Daniel it's your turn to be something."

Going over to his twin nephews Patrick took each child on his knee, "when are you two guys going to call me uncle instead of Unca."

Two pairs of eyes homed in to stare at this uncle. "Next year" Cameron replied. "Yes next year." echoed his brother Alistair.

"Okay you two why next year, what's the matter with now, today." asked their uncle with a smirk.

"Because we are just three, but next year we will be four," ended Cameron. "Yes and when we are nearly four we will say Uncle Patrick and Uncle Christopher but not Unca Aub" explained Alistair.

Before Patrick could ask the all important question why still Unca Aub the man himself leaned over and whispered; "they asked if they had to say Uncle Aubrey or would I like to stay Unca Aub."

"We said yes we liked Unca Aub best so we will have two uncles next year and one Unca Aub all the time; explained Cameron Then as an afterthought said, "We will keep our entire Auntie's just the same."

Having got that thorny subject sorted out the little boys wriggled down from Patrick's knees and went to inquire of Heather when was supper time because they were hungry.

Sebastian came over and taking a seat near his brother asked; "Did you and Lucy enjoy your day? While you were out we had a visitor or rather visitors, when we have finished supper if you both will join me in the small sitting room I will bring you both up to date. It's nothing we can't handle but I don't want Lucy to be worried."

"What do you mean Sebastian, why should Lucy be worried?

"Oh Hell, sorry Patrick I didn't mean to alarm you, I'm making a hash of this but, no Patrick please leave it until after supper. I must go and help Christina with the boys, bad timing on my part."

Taking his leave of his younger brother Sebastian felt like kicking himself for blurting out his worries like that. Patrick will have enough on his plate without him adding to them. He hadn't felt so helpless since that dreadful night when he thought he had lost Christina. He remembered those awful hours when he had no idea where she was. No he didn't feel quite that helpless. He knew he had the support of his family and this included Aubrey and Josephine and he also knew he could count on Kate and her professor Charles Blossom.

Passing the palm of his hand over his face Sebastian recalled he hadn't seen or heard from Kate since her late night dash to the rescue of Charles and his family. Once this holiday was over he must try and get back on track. This would include his young baby sister. He grinned to himself, some baby she would surely kill him if she knew he thought of her that way.

"Darling are you Okay, you look miles away. I think it's time for a little relaxing therapy. Once these two hooligans are in bed it will be your turn I promise," Christina leaned into her husband's arms. "We will have about an hour to ourselves just you and me." Christina turned towards her children. "Right you two it's bath-time then Daddy will tell you a SHORT story then its sleepy time."

Some time or rather some considerable time later, Sebastian and Christina joined the rest of the family just in time for a late supper.

Christopher was talking to Josephine, while Aubrey together with Daniel was entertaining Elizabeth and Patrick, leaving Lucy and Heather to entertain Fiona and Michael.

It was then Mr Benson struck the gong several times causing almost everybody in the large drawing room to place their collective hands over their ears.

"One day I am going to take that infernal Going out and bury it," muttered Elizabeth. "It is just for Christmas and Mr Benson gets so much pleasure from making sure we all hear it's meal time," soothed Daniel, and besides he sometimes lets me have a go."

"Alright I will leave it for now, but remind me to hide the striker before the next big family gathering."

"Ah yes love, speaking of family gatherings how many guests are we to expect for Kate and her professor's wedding? And have you any idea when this wedding is to take place?"

"Daniel your guess is as good as mine, but from what she told Christopher, and he told me, it will be sooner than later, in fact much sooner."

"Do you mean we have about as much time to make the arrangements as we did?" Elizabeth's spouse asked with a very mischievous grin.

"It was thirty five days yesterday now it's thirty four and counting." whispered his lady wife."Which means you had better get yourself organised my lad."

What she didn't say was there might be at least two new additions to the family. Of course she would not say a word until the ladies concerned had the pleasure of making their own announcement. However this was to be remedied in a short while.

As they all decided to take their coffee in the drawing room is was Patrick who started the ball rolling.

Looking around at the assembled members of his family Patrick beamed at them as he stood up.

"Lucy and I have a very special announcement to make." Going over to his wife he drew her to her feet and placing his arms around her, proudly announced.

"We, my lovely Lucy and I are going to have a baby who will be joining us in mid June. He or she will be another addition to the McKenzie family tree."

"This calls for more than coffee by way of celebration," turning towards his wife Daniel said "shall we crack open a bottle of Champagne especially as this is Patrick and Lucy's first?" but before Elizabeth could reply her eldest son spoke. Taking Christina's hand in his he looked around the room all of these people are family he thought, then smiling as though he had just won the lottery turned towards his brother.

"Patrick I am delighted with your news but as we are to celebrate a new arrival may I make the toast to New Arrivals?" Waiting just a beat Sebastian continued; "we are expecting a new baby due to arrive at the beginning of July, we haven't informed the boys yet, we think it's a little too early, but will wait until after Aunty Kate's wedding when things have quieted down a bit." As he sat down there was a burst of laughter. "Sebastian you have to be joking, when have things ever settled down in this family" his mother exclaimed.

By this time Heather returned to be followed by Mr Benson carrying two bottles of Champagne. Daniel handed round the glasses then holding his aloft said- "To my two dearly loved step sons and their lovely wives Lucy and Christina our heartiest congratulations."

Elizabeth was too emotional to speak she simply went to her boys and their wives and after kissing them, managed to say;

"This is the best news we could possibly have. There is going to be problems ahead for us in 1999 but thankfully nothing we cannot handle. Two new babies." her voice broke Daniel went to her and holding her close said very quietly;"Don't cry my darling, new babies is our future and what a wonderful future we shall have."

Aubrey was remembering what Lord Jeremy Tallington had once said to him. "It was time for Pipers Gate to have babies rolling round the floor."

Well to date there are four little ones with the promise of two more next year and if he knew his Josephine there might just be another one before the year ended. He did not leave Kate out of his equation but she may not have any babies if she and her professor decided to travel a bit first. But still two definite's and one maybe, wasn't bad odds.

Josephine noticed her husband's smile. "Well my boy if I guess correctly next Christmas would be just about right to introduce another McKenzie Page to the baby stakes." Taking a hold of his hand she gave it a short tug to get his attention. Aubrey bent down to hear what she was saying.

"How about a Christmas Page for next year?" A smile spread across his face, then a look a tenderness as he replied; "Sweetheart if you are game so am I, the more the merrier." If anyone noticed this little interplay between Aubrey and Josephine they didn't make any comment. So the day which had seen many surprises, some not pleasant, and some so wonderful the families retired for the night on a high.

CHAPTER 25

29TH DECEMBER 1998

Charles cornered Kate in the kitchen just after breakfast on the Wednesday morning.

"You and I need to talk, is there somewhere we can have a conversation that doesn't have anything to do with nephews, or nieces, new babies or injured Daddies. Do you know we haven't had a minute to ourselves since the evening of Boxing Day? Kate this has got to stop, you are working a fourteen hour day."

Holding up his hand to prevent her interrupting he continued. "You came at your great Aunt's behest and not once have I heard you either ask why I telephoned her or complained. You are being treated like a cross between the daily help and nanny all rolled into one."

Stopping to take a breath, Charles opened his mouth to continue with a list of all the things Kate was doing and not doing, but seemed to have run out of steam. Kate looked at him in admiration. My! My! He is on a roll and not wanting to break the list of items he needed to get of his chest, stood there waiting.

"Kate just look at you, looking as fresh as a daisy, but you should be with your family not letting the Blossom family run you ragged."

It was the last of Charles' list which really got Kate's dander up. Walking across the room, at the same time checking to make sure there were no children in the offing, Kate stood immediately in front of her irate new fiancé. Poking a finger into his chest she asked;

"Am I complaining? Are you suggesting I am not up to the job that needs to be done? Are you having second thoughts about our engagement? This by the way had to be conveyed to my family and yours by a third party instead of us together. Did you hear any complaint about driving here in the middle of the night in answer to your SOS to my great Aunt, and while we are on the subject of the said great Aunt how come it was to her you phoned for help in the first place?"

My God seeing his Kate hopping spitting mad was a sight to behold, even if her anger was directed to him. But for the life of him he couldn't understand the reason why she was so mad. He was only expressing his concern about how hard she was working for his brother's family.

Taking a deep breath and crossing his fingers and toes, Charles leaned forward and placing his mouth on hers whispered, "hush Princess, let us take time out and start this conversation again but this time somewhere quiet, just you and me eh!"

Leaning into his warm body Kate drew a shuddering breath."Sorry love you are quite right, we both need some time to ourselves, but until help arrives we will have to wait."

"Kate I have only just remembered my sister Ava is due home today sometime. She's been visiting our other side of the family in Tunisia, one set of Grandparents and two Aunts and their husbands. Oh My Good Lord, I was supposed to collect her dog from Kennels and I had promised to go to her house and turn the heating on. It's been off for four weeks."

"Charles don't panic what time is she due home?"

"Sometime this evening, round about eight-ish I think. I have it all written down back home in Long Melford."

"In that case I believe Christopher can help with the heating side of it. He is going back to London this morning. If I get a move on I will ask if he will collect the key from here and pop into your sister's place on his way to the M11, where does Ava actually live. I take it her house relatively close."

"Yes more or less straight down the road a bit, Number 12 Burleigh Street, just round the corner from the Burleigh Arcade, it's now a posh shopping Mall."

As Kate waited for Mr Benson to locate her brother she went over in her mind what Charles had just been complaining about. He was right to a certain extent, but she hadn't found it hard to look after Lauren and the children as well as Charles. Seeing the children interact with their mother and new baby brother was revealing in itself. She had taken on board how Lauren was handling Steve who inclined to be jealous of the newest addition to the Blossom family and Jessica who tended to be the bossy big sister. Perhaps she would be in the same position herself one day. Oh Lord how she hoped so. Her train of thought was interrupted by Christopher's voice asking what it was she wanted.

"How did you know I wanted anything?" She retorted.

"Because dear sister of mine its only nine-thirty in the morning, anyway love how can I help?"

"Hang on a minute Charles can explain better than I can." Handing the phone to Charles saying "you can give the precise instruction as to where the controls for the central heating are, and the precise address."

"Christopher, very well Christopher, once again I need your help." After explaining the reason for a further SOS Charles once again thanked his future Brother -in-law and hung up.

"Are we all going to Aunty Ava's house?" a voice called from the doorway?"

"No Jessica we are not going; Mr McKenzie is only calling here to collect the front door key, so he can let himself in to adjust her central heating before she arrives home later this evening."

After Christopher had collected the key and prior to departure, warned his sister he expected to see her, together with her very new finance on the 1st January 1999.

"Josephine and Aubrey are celebrating New Year with a family dinner at one o'clock sharp. All the family are coming from Pipers Gate on New Year's morning as this may well be the last all family gathering for a while."

"What do you mean Christopher McKenzie you cannot make a statement like that and just leave?"

Waving his hand called out with a grin; "Just Watch me." as he climbed into his sports car and drove off with a wave.

CHAPTER 26

The distance from Charles' house was approximately just over one mile but as Charles had explained parking was diabolical, if not impossible.

The narrow streets were not designed for modern living. The houses, a combination of late Victorian and early Edwardian made an eclectic mix and Ava Blossoms was a trim brick built Victorian dwelling with just a strip of land between the front-door and the footpath. Six steps led to the shiny black front-door with its big brass knocker as though it was waiting in eager anticipation for someone to give it a resounding knock.

In this instance Christopher knew it would have to remain silent as the owner was not expected to be home before he would be long gone.

However fate or whatever one chose to call it, sometimes grants you a gift of the unexpected, although at the time the recipient may not appreciate the gesture.

After spending what he considered more time than he wanted to or had envisaged Christopher finally inserted the key in the old fashioned brass keyhole. The door opened and trying to be careful not to trample on any mail which would have collected behind the door was more than surprised to find not one envelope or flyer. Miss Blossom must have arranged for a friend to call and collect her mail or perhaps left instructions with the post office to collect on her return from wherever she had been. Come to mention it her brother had not told Christopher where his sister was or rather where she had been.

He was just about to open the door leading down into the basement which housed the boiler, and the necessary thermostat which controlled the central heating, when he became aware someone or thing was immediately behind him. Before he could turn to see who or what it was he felt a blow to the back of his head then nothing.

It was black although not pitch black, but sort of a hazy swirling black mixed with a hint of grey, rather like a winter's evening dark mist.

The voice seemed to be coming from somewhere to his right. More than one voice, it was sort of a babble nothing coherent, then a light voice called for silence. The pitch was low but quite clear. It said "will you all please be quiet; I do not think he is dead, but unfortunately his head looks as though he needs hospital attention. Does anyone know exactly what happened?"

"Please Miss Blossom it was me. I had just come from the back of the house when I saw this man opening the door to the basement. I thought you were not due to be home before seven this evening, so I knew he couldn't be here to see you. He looked like a burglar from behind so I hit him with the vase from the hall table. Is he dead Miss? I didn't mean to hit him so hard; and if he is dead it's my fault."

"No Mandy he is not dead thank God, but from the look of him when he wakes up he is going to have a monumental headache. I think I know who he is. However, we had better get him to somewhere more comfortable than where he is at present. Are any of the boys in residence yet? Right then be a good girl and go find two of the biggest ones and tell them I need them here."

The grey began to lift a little, sharp stabbing pains flashed behind Christopher's eyes. Ye Gods his head hurt. Unable to stifle a groan Christopher felt rather than saw a cool hand feel his brow, and a soothing voice telling him he would be more comfortable in a little while.

"I don't have a little while to waste lying here on your floor." he whispered "I should be on my way to London; Jim Harris is expecting me to arrive early after-noon."

"Mr McKenzie you are not going anywhere until the doctor arrives and examines the wound to your head."

Lifting his hand to feel that very painful part of his anatomy he almost shouted Ouch! His hair appeared to be sticky with something.

The owner of the soothing voice took a hold of his exploring hand and taking it between her own said, "Mr McKenzie, the doctor will here in a few minutes try and keep your head still until he arrives."

"Well Ava my dear where is this young man you have almost managed to kill?"

Before Ava could answer Christopher once again felt rather than saw a pair of hands examining his injury.

"That's a nasty cut you have laddie, but once we get you cleaned up and into somewhere more comfortable we can then see the full extent of the damage."

With those reassuring words the doctor then gave crisp directions to the two young men waiting to assist Christopher to a more suitable place to attend to the wound on his head.

"It is a good thing you have a very thick thatch of hair, plus of course a good solid scull, you will have to have a couple sutures, but once the headache clears up you should be a right as rain. I will leave something for the pain but after a couple of hours you can go home. I suggest you get someone to drive you. Take things slowly for a bit and if the headache has not cleared the end of the week pop yourself into Addenbrooks A&E. Good Day and A Happy New Year to you Miss Blossom."

Christopher opened his eyes very slowly he was lying on what used to be called a day bed in a dimly lit room. The curtains where drawn against the winter afternoon, he couldn't see what was in the room other a couple of fireside chairs either side of the hearth. Turning his head was a No! No! .it hurt too much. His mouth felt dry, he desperately needed a drink, something cold, and lots of it. As though guessing his need someone rose from one of the chairs and crossing over to him asked if he would like some assistance in sitting up. ."Just give me your hand I can manage the rest." Suiting actions to words Christopher struggled to sit while at the same time trying to keep his head from moving. After a two false starts he managed to swing his legs round and off the sofa to sit up straight, the effort made him sweat.

Waiting until her uninvited guest was vertical Ava handed him a glass of water.

"Take a drink of this then I will get you some tea and if you feel like eating, a small toasted tea-cake. It must be sometime since you have eaten."

Christopher raised his eyes and for the first time saw the face the lovely soothing voice belonged to.

Although two years older than her brother Charles, Ava Blossom, now in her mid thirties was as lovely as when she had been in her early twenties.

Her hair cut close to her head like a dark silk cap topped a perfectly oval face slightly tinted as though she had been out in the sun, clear silver blue eyes under arched dark eyebrows all this atop of a slender figure with legs almost to her neck as Christopher was to describe them later to Patrick.

"Thank you yes please I would like that, but before you do will you please telephone your brother Charles, my sister is with him, and my family will be worried as will Jim Harris at our London House, I was supposed to be there by mid-afternoon."

"It is all being taking care of I telephoned my brother to tell him I was home earlier than expected so he didn't need to turn on the heating after all.

Now let me ring for tea and teacakes, one of my lodgers will attend to it. Young Mandy wanted to sit and hold your hand, she feels dreadful about laying you out cold. I think she envisaged being arrested for at least attempted murder and spending the rest of the holiday in the local *Nick*."

Taking on board what his hostess was saying Christopher picked up on her reference to the local police station.

"Are you in the police force?" he asked while sincerely hoping she was not.

"Not at all, I am a solicitor doing Pro Bona work /Legal Aid. Most of my clients are either going to or coming from the local magistrates' court or crown court. I have a regular clientele most weekends, mostly drunk and disorderly. Reasonably harmless and usually a night in the cells is enough to deter some of the younger ones."

As Ava finished her explanation Mandy returned with a tray of buttered teacakes and a large pot of tea.

Giving Christopher a shy smile said, "Sam is bringing the cups and saucers, and Declan has the rest of the tea things."

Two young men tall and built like two forward props for the local Rugby team were surprisingly light on their feet and extremely careful when handling the delicate china tea cups.

"Thank you both for assisting me from the basement stairs. When I fell it must have been head first straight down."

"Mr McKenzie I'm so sorry, I didn't mean to hit your so hard, and it's all my fault you are still here and not home where you should. Miss Blossom said you were on your way to London and only stopped by to do her a good turn. Then I went and nearly killed you. If I had, Doctor Jo would have been ever so upset and would not want me to see her any-more." Christopher was amazed, what had his sister got to do with him having an accident, because that's all it was. A very painful accident and apart from having a monumental headache and a few stitches in his scalp he reckoned he would live.

The younger of the two men pulled Mandy into a hug.

"Hush you silly chump, Mr McKenzie is going to be just fine and I'm sure Dr Jo will not say anything to you. Now dry your eyes, then you and me and perhaps Declan will go to collect Miss Blossom's dog."

Giving a final sniff Mandy gave Ava and Christopher a watery smile.

"Will you telephone the kennels and tell them we are on our way to collect Chessca."

In five minutes flat the room was once again quiet. Leaning back Christopher felt a sense of relief, his head still pounded and all he wanted was to close his eyes and sleep. As he drifted off he wondered what kind of dog was called *Chessca*, he must remember to ask Miss Blossom after he had a little rest. But Christopher McKenzie didn't wake up for a very long time and when he finally did, it was once again in totally different surroundings.

CHAPTER 27

Daniel Gibson took the call.

"Professor Gibson, my name is Doctor Lewis, consultant Neurologist at Addenbrooks. We have a member of your family, a Mr Christopher McKenzie he was admitted about an hour ago with a serious head wound sustained sometime this morning or early afternoon. Will you please inform his mother Mrs Elizabeth McKenzie Gibson his condition is extremely serious? We do have some private accommodation for close family and relatives but only two members of the family may see him at once. He is quite poorly but we are doing our very best for Christopher."

Daniel took a moment to gather his thoughts then replied.

"Dr Lewis I believe I have heard about you and perhaps met you. Are you connected to The National in Queen Square?" But before the said Doctor could reply Daniel continued "this is going to be a terrible shock to my wife and the rest of the family. Yes we will be with you inside the hour, thank you for calling me and not Elizabeth."

Hanging up the phone Daniel took a minute to collect his thoughts. How could he tell his beloved wife her youngest son was in hospital with a serious head injury? Miss Blossom had telephoned her brother telling him the doctor had been and said Christopher was going to OK. Charles had telephoned the family at Pipers Gate and told them Christopher had had an accident but was going to be alright, and now he wasn't going to be alright.

Dear God he had only had this young man as his son for such a short time. Taking a deep breath Daniel went back into the large drawing room and quietly going to his wife's side asked her to accompany him to Grandpa's study.

"Daniel is something the matter my dear you look dreadfully pale. Are you feeling ill? Come and sit down I will call Dr Marshall."

Taking her hands Daniel replied with just a hitch to his voice, "Elizabeth, my dear it's Christopher, he has been admitted to Addenbrooks Neurological block, we have to go at once, his condition is causing some concern. They have sent for his family or rather those who wish to come."

He choked back a sob, it's no use my getting all upset I have to hang on in there for my family. How strange, he had known the McKenzie children almost since they had been born, and for some strange reason had taken it for granted that in some strange way they partly belonged to him. It had taken the imminent loss of one to bring home to him, in his mind they were his, each and everyone was very precious to him. It was his son fighting for his life, and he would see the Devil himself in Hell before he allowed him to die. All this passed through Daniels mind in a flash.

Elizabeth gave one long shuddering sob as her husband drew her into his arms. Holding her close for moment then Elizabeth raised her head.

"Daniel we have to go now right this minute but first I must tell the family they have to right to know how serious this is. I will leave Sebastian and Heather to make whatever arrangements for the family to come.

Returning to the family, gathered together just days after Christmas and preparing for the New Year, was the hardest thing Elizabeth had to do since that first time after Skye McKenzie had been killed.

As soon as their mother re-entered the room the noise seemed to stop without anyone knowing why; intuition perhaps? No one could say but that frisson of something stopped the various conversations.

"Ma what's going on, what's happened? Sebastian spoke first, Christina went to his side took a hold of his hand waiting.

Clearing her throat she opened her mouth but she found she couldn't speak her throat was clogged with tears. Straightening her back she started again.

"Daniel has taken a telephone call from Addenbrookes. Christopher is in critical care in the Neurological unit. The doctor said we should go as my boy." her voice hitched "my son and your brother Christopher is seriously ill. The accident he suffered this morning is more serious than the doctor, who saw him earlier today thought a first. That's all we know. Daniel and I are going right now. If any of you want to come later there will be a room set aside for his family."

Daniel returned carrying his wife's top coat and a small case with toilet necessities for an overnight stay. Stopping as he reached the doorway said, "I will telephone you immediately when we have spoken to Doctor Lewis, he is the consultant in charge. Try not to worry too much; I think if you all say a Prayer together it may help.

For a moment the only sound breaking the silence was the sound of Daniels car fading as he and Christopher's mother set off towards Cambridge.

The first sound was not a cry or a sob but a firm voice announcing:

"Mr Benson is bringing in some hot tea, some sandwiches and cakes then we are going to plan a campaign. This will make it easier for you all to visit your brother without all arriving in one go.

As soon as Professor Daniel phones and gives us all a clear picture of what we have to face we will be prepared. Your mother will cope as she has done before, but she will still need to know we are all here for her. So you must prepare a working rota to enable you to visit without treading on each other's feet. As for me, I too have trodden this path before and I love Christopher as if he was my own son but we cannot help him to recover if we let our emotions get in the way of common sense. I will go and chase up Mr Benson." as she finished speaking Heather's voice broke and she hurried of before anyone tried to comfort her because she knew if she started crying she would never stop.

It Was Aubrey who stepped out to help Mr Benson pour out the tea and Lucy hand round the cups and saucers. No one seemed inclined to eat any of the food set before them.

Aubrey paused beside his wife and taking her hands in his bent to kiss her cheek, then after what appeared to be a short conversation once again stood to face the assembled people in the room.

"As you all know Church House big enough to transfer the whole of our branch of the McKenzie clan. You are all very welcome to come and stay with us until Christopher is on the mend." He could not contemplate his young brother-in-law dying.

"We have a trained children's Nanny, Miriam who loves all small people to bits, I am sure she will be happy to include Alistair and Cameron.

We also have Mrs Brice to help out. Of course Heather will come with us. I will ask Mr Benson if he will hold the fort here. We, who all know and love Christopher, will be there for him however long it takes."

"Thank you Aubrey and Josephine, I think your proposal is a great idea as I'm sure the rest of you do to. Once we know the score from Daniel we will prepare to remove ourselves to take up your very kind offer and move to Church House en masse.

Later in the privacy of their room Christina stood behind her husband massaging his neck, "Darling I am so proud of you, not once did you play the blame game. Kate will be devastated, as stated she will be blaming herself for suggesting Christopher call on Charles Blossom's sister. We have got to help her cope with this trauma. It's taken thirteen long years to get her home for any length of time. As for Charles Blossom what his feelings are at the moment, I cannot imagine."

CHAPTER 27

Christina was spot on with her analysis of Kate. When Ava Blossom telephoned her brother early in the day to explain what had happened to Christopher she assured them that Kate's brother had sustained an accident over a case of mistaken identity, but the Doctor had said not to worry it was a minor injury, mostly a cut to the head and some bruising, but hopefully he would be fine in a couple of days. She had then gone to explain she had returned home twenty-four hours earlier than she had previously arranged. She would explain when they all met up later.

"The accident happened because one of my lodgers thought Mr McKenzie was a bugler."

"What Lodgers, if you have lodgers why in the name of heaven didn't you arrange for one of them to put the heating on. Please don't use the excuse you forgot or didn't have time. My only hope is Christopher makes a full recovery and doesn't decide to sue you, you hare brained idiot."

"I will telephone you later when you are in a better frame of mind. Please give my sincere apologies to Miss McKenzie." responded a very uptight Miss Blossom.

Charles very carefully replaced the receiver, then taking Kate's hand in his pulled her close.

"What can I say love, other than I am so sorry, I should have left the flaming heating, we have more than enough on our plate than to run after a member of my family who can be so self centred at times."

"Charles you must stay and see to things here, the doctors said they will let us know what is happening to Keith later today. But I must go to Christopher he should have been taken to hospital right away. I only hope the GP who has seen him is right in his diagnosis. As soon as I have seen my brother I will telephone and bring you up to date."

In just a matter of minutes Kate was on her way.

She spotted her brother's car parked just a short way from the house, she wasn't so lucky it was quite a good fifteen minutes before she presented herself at Number 12. Looking for a door bell she was obliged to give the knocker two sharp raps. The door was opened and what at first looked like a little girl peered out.

"Yes."

"I'm Dr Kate McKenzie I have come to see my brother, I believe he is still here?"

"Yes but the doctor has been and said Mr McKenzie is going to get well again, soon I think."

"May I come in?" At the same time stepping into the hall. "Will you take me to where he is?"

"Hello, do come inside." a voice said from a doorway to her right. Kate turned to see who she was speaking to. Holding out her hand she introduced herself to the figure standing in the open doorway.

"I'm Dr Katherine McKenzie, Christopher is my brother I am here to see him."

"How do you do was the formal response I am Miss Ava Blossom. If you will come this way, the doctor said Mr McKenzie was to rest and once his headache clears up he will make a full recovery."

However, what greeted Kate was not a brother who was a bit sorry for himself with a severe headache. Although not a doctor of medicine Kate had lived in the house of a country GP and with her sister whilst studying for a medical degree to know when something was wrong.

"Gently lifting one of his eyelids she noted the pupil was dilated checking the other one it was the same. Christopher moaned.

"Kate what's happening to me I have a terribly pain in my head, I feel peculiar floating cannot concentrate, should be going to London. Am I in London now, must talk to Jim. Jim Harris where is he?" He paused then tried to sit up but instead was violently sick.

Turning to the silent woman beside her Kate issued two words.

"Paramedics Now." turning back to Christopher grabbed the first thing she could lay hands on which happened to be porcelain fruit bowl .Gently supporting Christopher's head until he stopped. Laying his head very carefully back on the cushion she decided she would save her questions to Miss Ava Blossom until her brother was safely in hospital. The Ambulance arrived almost immediately, and after a quick and very thorough examination, Christopher was transferred to Addenbrooks A & E within minutes. Kate followed in her car and it was only when she arrived at their destination she realized, she had not thought to ask Miss Blossom to accompany her.

Miss Ava Blossom after giving her lodgers a few terse instructions followed the ambulance just minutes after it left.

Fortunately the traffic was light but finding a place to park was a nightmare. Addenbrooks Hospital was notorious for its parking arrangement. It's very size almost intimidating at the best of times. So when finding a parking space as close to A & E became an almost impossibility Kate drove straight into a reserved place allocated to some unknown doctor. If the said doctor complained she would deal with him or her later.

Seeing Kate McKenzie's car Ava parked alongside. Now two cars were technically illegally parked up.

Ava saw Kate almost immediately, she was listening very intently to someone in a white coat most likely a consultant to her brother.

Kate stood perfectly still, then nodding her head several times turned slightly and catching sight of Ava Blossom beckoned her over.

Half turning she said by way of introduction. "This is Miss Blossom she was the first person on the scene after my brother suffered a severe blow to the head by one of her lodgers who mistook him for a burglar. I am quite sure it was an accident but she should have called for the paramedics and not taken upon herself to consider his injuries did not warrant hospital attention."

If Charles' sister had felt dreadful about the accident before Kate's scathing comments about her seemed lack of concern, it would hard to imagine how she felt now.

"Miss McKenzie it was not lack of concern or want of care, your brother Mr McKenzie insisted he felt fine apart from a headache. Surely you must know if he had shown the slightest signs of confusion or sickness |I would have got help at once."

Kate giving her a cold look replied; "I don't think you have known my brother more than a few minutes therefore your assessment of his condition is questionable and the name is Professor Katherine McKenzie," she added as a rider.

"My apologies Professor McKenzie, you are of course quite right in your assumptions. I do not know Mr McKenzie to form any kind of opinions relating to either his health or well-being. However because a member of my household is responsible for the situation in which he finds himself I will of course accept total responsibility for any expenses and compensation.

I would like to remain here until the doctors have diagnosed the problems and if I may see him before I go I will be grateful." the last word was more of a sob than a request.

Kate turned and taking her hand without saying one word drew her forward towards the room set aside for the family.

Both young women were sitting side by side still holding hands as though each willing the other to do something rather than this awful waiting and listening to the silence.

After what seemed hours of waiting, the door opened quietly to admit one Professor Daniel and Mrs Elizabeth Gibson.

"Mum, Daniel, have you any news? We." waving her hand Kate indicated Ava, "have been here hours and all they nurses keep telling us is the *doctors as still with him but they will tell us what's happening in a little while,* but that was ages ago."

Daniel stepped forward and gathered the sobbing woman into his arms.

"Hush now Kate, this is not like you to get into a state just because you have to wait and cannot have an instant answer. Come now my lovely, come and sit by me and I will try to fill you both in."

Nodding his head towards Ava, "you must Charles' sister, I am Kate's Step-Papa, now you come and sit alongside Kate then I can tell you both what has happened and what is happening right now."

Holding out his hand he took Elizabeth's thus making a small intimate circle.

Christopher has a blood-clot inside his head about the size of a ten penny piece and is pressing on the soft tissue of his brain. This is causing the pain and the disorientation and vomiting. If the clot is left any longer it may burst and could cause irreversible damage. Therefore Dr Lewis is of the opinion that this must be removed at once.

Fortunately a senior Neurological consultant is available on the premises and is preparing to what is termed *excise this clot* from Christopher's brain as we speak."

Daniel rose to his feet and gathered his wife into his arms as he spoke.

"Hold on fast sweetheart our boy will make it. Remember we are all praying for him, not just us here, but all the McKenzie clan. You know what you tell me." Looking directly into her eyes, he waited.

"Hang on in there, keep the faith and all will be well." she whispered in reply. Then burying her head against his shoulder she started to sob.

"Daniel what will I do if he." she could not bring herself to say those dreadful words aloud.

"No he will get better love just wait a little while longer and I am sure the news will be good." Daniel crossed his fingers and just hoped to God he was right.

CHAPTER 28

After what seemed to be half a lifetime a member of the team from ICU came softly into the room where Daniel and Elizabeth were waiting with Kate and Ava. Going over to Elizabeth and Daniel spoke quietly to them both.

Kate unable to hear what she said saw her mother put her hands to her face, and as Daniel gathered her close she began to sob, great tearing sobs, as though she had been saving them up for some dreadful occasion.

The nurse seeing Kate's look of concern, fear and confusion, all rolled into one crossed over to the two young women to explain.

"I have just explained to your parents your brother has had the operation and so far as we know it has been successful. At present he is back in ICU in a drug induced coma, this is to allow the brain to recover. We will know more in a little while. We cannot give you a date when this will be but every effort will be made to ensure he is as comfortable as possible.

You and your family may visit whenever you wish but," the nurse held up her hand,

"Mr Duffy Christopher's consultant has stated at present only two visitors at a time. At first just hold his hand and make no attempt to rouse him. When his consultant Mr Kenneth Duffy decides to bring Christopher out of his coma he will tell you all what he expects from you. I have explained to you mother Christopher is young and healthy and Mr Duffy expects him to make a full recovery." Going back to Daniel and Elizabeth she indicated she was now ready to take to them to see their son.

The darkness outside seemed to cocoon the occupants inside the small room allocated to the McKenzie family during their long wait. No one was talking; it was as though they were all suspended in time.

The door opened, and without a sound been uttered those present all rose to their feet as one.

Crossing to where his mother was seated holding Daniels hand as though her life depended on it Sebastian whispered, "Any news Ma?" Patrick and Lucy and my Christina are outside in the corridor waiting to take their turn to sit with Christopher for ten minutes."

Daniel rose to his feet. "Let us go outside and I will bring you up to date." Bending down to kiss his wife Daniel murmured "I'll be back in just a few minutes love."

Sebastian followed his Step-Papa out into the corridor only to be surrounded by his wife, brother, and sister -in-law who asked in almost one voice. "What's happening and how is Christopher? How is?" but before the last question could be finished Mr Kenneth Duffy joined them.

Holding out his hand he introduced himself. "I'm Kenneth Duffy Neurological Consultant to your brother." Nodding his head to the two McKenzie men stated rather than asked. "You are Christopher's brothers."

"I'm Sebastian and this is our middle brother Patrick, this lady is my wife Christina."

"Patrick and my wife Lucy McKenzie," responded Patrick.

Looking from one face to another Kenneth Duffy saw the same fear and concern as he had when he first met the other McKenzie's, but this time he was in a position to give the family some hope.

"Your brother suffered a severe blow to the head just behind his right ear, at first there didn't appear to be much damage and even if he had been admitted to hospital immediately, there would at that stage nothing see apart from a slight swelling and a nasty bruise. It was only later there was evidence of a blood clot forming which in turn was pressing on the membrane of his brain. This is called an *Intra-Axial Haematoma*. Fortunately your other sister Katherine was quick to recognise the signs of a cranial disturbance and sought help at once. In my opinion she played a major part in saving Christopher's life.

I together with members of my team, have operated on your brother by making an incision in his head slightly above the swelling and have excised the blood clot without damaging the brain membrane. However I have explained to your parents Christopher is not out of the woods yet, the next few days will be critical.

At present he is in a drug induced coma, this will assist the swelling and bruising to heal. Plus this will hopefully prevent a sudden *Brain Haemorrhage*. I, together with my team will monitor your brother, and do all in our power to ensure his comfort and care.

In the meantime I would suggest you all go home and get some rest.

Professor and Mrs Gibson are going to stay through the night."

Shaking each hand in turn Mr Duffy left them to themselves to decide who goes home and who would stay with their parents.

Despite Mr Duffy explaining to Elizabeth and Daniel there was little they could do for the next little while Elizabeth insisted she was not moving until she was satisfied her son was not going to die.

"Come here love, sit by me and just let me hold you." Daniel murmured.

The two brothers were allowed in to see their kid brother for five minutes, then before returning to the relative's room it was decided Patrick would take the two ladies back to Pipers Gate until morning, he would then return after assisting with the general move to Church House.

Rejoining Elizabeth and the rest of the group Sebastian conveyed the conversation they had had with Mr Duffy.

"Mr Duffy has suggested there is nothing we can do for Christopher tonight other than sit beside his bed, so I am going to stay here with you and Daniel Ma, and the rest of you are to go home. Patrick is going to take Lucy and Christina back to Pipers Gate to help with the general packing up prior to going to Church House. Aubrey and Josephine are at present holding the fort together with Heather.

In the morning I am going to take you both to Aubrey and Dr Jo who will be there to look after you."

Elizabeth looked across the room at her eldest son. "Sebastian I am not going anywhere until I know my boy is definitely getting better."

"No Ma." Sebastian crossed the floor in a couple of strides. "Just for once allow yourself the luxury of being comforted and loved by Daniel. We are going to have some long days and nights before Christopher is out of the woods." Kissing his mother once again Sebastian rose to his feet at the same time ushering out those who were going back to Pipers Gate, albeit reluctantly.

CHAPTER 29

By the time Patrick with his wife and sister-in-law had given an account of the state of affairs regarding Christopher's condition it was almost dawn.

"You two ladies are going to bed with a hot-water bottle apiece and as for you Patrick you look dead on your feet. I have everything ready to make your breakfast then a good sleep and later this after-noon we will be ready to be transported to Church House.

Mr Benson has already organised the luggage and has promised the twins they may ride in his car. He is going to drive the Professor's four wheel drive. He cleared it with Daniel when we telephoned just after you and the ladies left."

While Heather had been talking, she had at the same time heated up enough soup to fill three large bowls. Serving this at the kitchen table with warm bread fresh from the bread-maker she insisted all three ate before retiring to catch up on their sleep.

"Heather will you please call us if there is any change in Christopher's condition. I know we cannot do anything but pray and wait." continued Christina, "but as a family we all need to be." her voice broke; "together," she ended on a sob. Inside she was aching for her husband, to offer him comfort and support. Also for Elizabeth, who had just found happiness again with Daniel in the autumn of their lives. Surely after all Elizabeth had gone through, God would not be so unkind as to take her youngest son from her.

Turning to Heather Lucy put her arms around her. "Keep the faith Heather, all will be well and thank you for being here for us, feeding us and now chasing us off to bed."

As Lucy and Christina headed for bed each lady clutching a hot-water bottle; Patrick turned back and gathering Heather to him just cuddled her in. "Get some rest love, we are all in this together." then kissing her very gently on the mouth whispered I do love you, lots."

It was Mr Benson who took the call from Addenbrooks before anyone was up.

"Mr Benson, there is no need to disturb the family this is just an interim report." Daniel tried to sound upbeat but couldn't keep the weariness from his voice as he continued. "Christopher is still unconscious but is holding his own. The consultant said he will keep him in a drug induced coma for another twenty-four hours. Then providing there is no deterioration, the amount of drugs will be gradually reduced, thus allowing Christopher to regain consciousness within the following two days. All we can do for the next little for the while is to watch and pray.

I am going to take Elizabeth directly to Church House, Aubrey left a message for us when he telephoned early this morning to say everything is ready for the whole family as and when they arrive. Apparently Mrs Brice and Miriam have been up since first light getting everything organised.

Once again I must thank you Mr Benson for taking over the complete running of Piper Gate at such short notice, we are very grateful." .

After reassuring Daniel Pipers Gate would be safe in his hands Mr Benson went to find Heather to pass on the message. But for once he did not find a sensible down to earth housekeeper, but a lady in distress. It was very obvious she had been crying and with no one to see her Heather had given in to the terrible grief in her heart. She had always treated the children equally, but Christopher was special. As a little four year old the first person he saw when he first came home to his Grandpa Drummond's house was Heather. Holding out her arms to a frightened little child, she gathered him to her saying. "I've got you sweetheart don't cry, you are safe now, Heather won't let anything harm you." Then taking him on her lap she sang to him a lullaby she used to sing to another little boy, not so long ago.

CHAPTER 30

While all drama was being played out at Addenbrooks Hospital, Charles Blossom had been tied up with his sister-in-law's parents. They had arrived shortly after midday in a flurry of greetings together with a list of questions starting from the accident to an up to date resume of what was to happen next. However all Charles could think of was his beloved Kate was somewhere together with his hapless sister without him. It was his fault Christopher McKenzie was fighting for his life.

All he wanted to do was to be with his Kate, to hold her hand and to offer her his support .But would she want him beside her; when he was indirectly the cause of her brother's injury.

Charles telephoned Pipers Gate very early the following morning where Heather brought him up to date with latest news from the hospital.

"Heather." he asked hesitating before continuing. "Do you think Kate will ever forgive me? It was all my fault, if I hadn't asked Christopher to put my sister's central heating on he would not be fighting for his life."

Heather didn't waste time with the usual platitudes or words of false sympathy.

"Dr Charles Blossom, it was an accident, with hindsight it could no doubt have been avoided, but Christopher is in safe hands and your place is where you are until Lauren's parents arrive. Later today the family are to move into Church House. The Judge and Josephine are already there making the necessary preparations. Once you are free from your present responsibilities ring Church House, find out where Kate is then you can join her. One thing I would advise, handle her with great care she has a habit of withdrawing into herself, giving the impression she doesn't care one way or another, but Charles, she does care, very deeply. The cocksure attitude she shows to the world is a cover, especially when she has been very badly hurt. Not necessarily physically but mentally."

"You mean like she was so hurt by Jamie Tallington, she told me Heather, what he did to her all those years ago."

"Yes; but this time she has your loving support, go to her Dr Blossom and don't let her push you away."

With Heather's advice in the forefront of his mind Charles telephoned Church House. It was Kate herself who answered.

"Church House can I help you?" Kate's light contralto voice came over the phone.

"Kate may I come over and see you, no not see you but to hold you, comfort you." his voice broke he feared he was going to cry. Kate didn't reply straight away and Charles found he was praying under his breath. "Please God make her say yes I cannot go through losing her again, we have just found each other after almost three and a half years."

Kate heard the catch in Charles voice he sounds very upset.

"Charles I was afraid to call you in case something bad would happen to Christopher while I was away talking to you. I know it's silly but fear makes us do or in my case   do silly things. Darling how soon can you get here? I was going to catch up on my sleep but I will wait until you arrive."

Charles lost no time in explaining to Lauren the latest report from Pipers Gate.

"Charles you have done more than your share of duty here and you must stop beating yourself up about what has happened. It's been a terrible time for everybody concerned but its time you went to Kate. She loves you to bits. So don't go and spoil it all with a big dose of guilt." she smiled to take the sting out of her words.

She knew the Blossom men very well, loving, generous, and very kind but inclined to take their responsibilities very seriously with no allowances for not achieving their own high standards.

Oh Lord how she missed her beloved Keith, but sometime soon they would know the results of all the tests at present being carried out by the Orthopaedic team, also at Addenbrooks, there's nothing like keeping it in the family she thought with a wry smile.

CHAPTER 31

Mrs Brice opened the front door to find one Professor Charles Blossom standing on the doorstep.

"Good afternoon Professor please come this way Miss McKenzie is in the Library, I was about to take her a pot of tea." As she turned to lead the way a chorus of very young voices together with some older ones could be heard coming from the direction of the soon to be music room.

"Shall we try once again, are you ready? Here we go then. All things bright and beautiful. What's that Oliver? Come here poppet and I will help with the hard bits."

Charles was surprised, not just surprised but astonished and amazed. His sister was known for her lack of patience and so far as Charles was aware had not had very much to do with children, especially as young as the McKenzie and Page brood. Well! Well! That was indeed a turn up for the books.

He was still pondering over the change in his sister as Mrs Brice opened Library door at the same time announcing ; "Professor Blossom for you Miss McKenzie." But before she had finished speaking Charles had crossed the room and taking one astonished lady into his arms said, "I love you Kate McKenzie and will until the end of time." Bending his head he kissed her lightly on the lips, then holding her tight against him murmuring "forgive me darling for inadvertently causing you and your family so much distress."

At first Kate was just pleased to have her Charles close to her at long last. The passed thirty-six hours had been a nightmare, and if that was any indication of how life would be without Charles Fitzroy Blossom she wanted none of it.

Turning her face into his shoulder she gave a shuddering sob, this was followed by another and soon all the pent up grief and worry poured out in a flood of tears.

Charles stood and held on to her, allowing her time to cry as long as she needed, he was just devoutly thankful it was he offering his Kate the comfort she was in need of.

Finally when Kate's tears were shed, she accepted the handkerchief offered by Charles and after scrubbing her face to wipe away the remnants of her distress, she looked up and with shake in her voice said "Oh lord how I've missed you and wanted you."

With a hiccough she continued, "Christopher is not quite out of the woods yet but his consultant has said he is almost sure there is no brain damage. He may suffer from loss of memory relating to how he came to be in hospital but hopefully will make a complete recovery. Your sister has taken Christopher's accident personally, and has begged Aubrey to allow her to stay here until Christopher is fully conscious and well on the way to recovery."

Looking at her beloved Charles continued "your sister is making herself useful in more ways than one. Someone was needed to help entertain the small fry while their mothers had a rest. Ava volunteered, although she did say she knew next nothing about babies and small children she was willing it give a bash."

Kate giggled."There was a rush to accept her offer, although Miriam said she would help but Ava said Miriam needed her rest in order cope the little ones later."

Charles laughed both in relief and delight."Yes I heard her as I came in, she was trying to teach them All things bright and beautiful, but apparently Oliver was having difficulty with beautiful."

"Oh I am quite sure she will manage she is a very resourceful lady." Turning her face up to Charles, Kate kissed him gently on the lips.

"This feels just right."

Sometime later as the afternoon sunlight turned to dusk and the first stars joined the evening star in an indigo coloured sky, the telephone shattered the quiet serenity in the hall. There was a rush of feet to answer, then a short silence.

"Are you quite sure? Aubrey queried in a husky voice. "What did the consultant say? That is good news I will tell everyone here. You are going to Pipers Gate first then coming here later this evening. Why don't you come straight here and stay until morning then go to Pipers Gate. Yes of course I understand we seem to have lost track of time these past few days.

Yes I will pass on the good news, see you all soon."

By this time most of the household had gathered in the hall of Church House, so it was with a mile wide smile which embraced them all, Aubrey passed on the glad tidings.

"Christopher had regained consciousness just a little while ago and asked for a cup of tea, not too strong with two spoons of sugar. Elizabeth and Daniel are going to Pipers Gate straight from the hospital and will then come here later this evening. This will mean we shall all be together to see in the New Year , then later celebrate our New Year's Day dinner, which you all know is at one o'clock sharp."

Gathering his wife into his arms Aubrey held her close."Darling all is going to be OK let's collect our little ones it will soon be their bed time."

The sense of relief was almost palpable, but fate had one more surprise in store for the residents of Church House before the close 1998.

CHAPTER 32

31ST DECEMBER 1998.

"Dr Jo, may I speak to you in private?" Miriam Kahn stood just inside the door of Josephine's office waiting to be invited into the only room in the house which was strictly off limits to all the residents of Church House. Even Aubrey knocked before entering.

Glancing towards the source of the interruption Josephine noted Miriam seemed a little tense, as though she expected her to say something along the lines of *come back when I am not so busy.* "Yes of course Miriam is it about the children? Young Freddie is looking better this morning, his mouth is no longer so sore."

"No Doctor Jo, I would like your permission to visit Mr Christopher, just for a short time and I promise I will not stay too long and tire him out. I heard the judge telling everybody Mr Christopher has now regained consciousness and asked for a cup of tea with two sugars. He always has too much sugar in his tea and coffee, despite me explaining it was bad for him."

Taking on board what Miriam had just said Josephine filed it away to think about later. It was obvious her youngest brother and Miriam were friends, and during the last few days the family had been so engrossed with Christopher's accident and subsequent trauma, no one had noticed Miriam Kahn had withdrawn into herself. Miriam was part of the Aubrey-Page household, respected and cared for by the adults and loved by Oliver and Freddie. She also cared for Christina's little boys as and when all the McKenzie children where together.

The Brice boys thought she was great, she could and did tell wonderful stories, and sometimes she would have the children act out some of the stories. At present or until recent events had her put her schedule on hold, they had been all doing the voices from Tales of the Riverbank.

"I think it's a good idea Miriam, it will do him good to have someone who is not a family member, but how will you get there? Perhaps you could go with Kate and Ava immediately after Lunch?"

"Thank you but I do not wish to intrude, I will have to wait and go another day."

The young woman turned to go but before she got to the door Josephine had noted the fleeting expression on her face, as though someone had turned the light out of her eyes, leaving a deep seated pain almost too hard to bear.

"Miriam, can you arrange to go later this afternoon at about five o'clock, I will arrange for a Taxi to take you and bring you back when you are ready."

"I will be ready and promise to be home in time to see to the children's bedtime. Thank you so much you are very kind," Miriam said quietly, she had to get away before disgracing herself by bursting into tears of relief. These last few days had been a nightmare for her to keep a tight rein on her feelings.

The taxi arrived on the stroke of five o'clock as promised. And had anyone seen Miriam prior to leaving for Addenbrooks, they would not have recognised the glowing young woman dressed as though she was going on a date with her lover, not quite a date but to see and to hold the person she loved.

Christopher was lying propped up with several pillows with his eyes closed, hearing the soft footfall approaching the bed his eyes shot open, "Miriam" holding out his hands he made to hold her but due to various drips and apparatus attached to his arms was unable to do so. Taking his hands Miriam bent over and kissed him so gently it felt as though he was been touched by a butterfly.

"Christopher I have been so worried, no that is the wrong word, terrified, I so wanted to come to you, to hold you, to kiss the pain away. I promise myself I would not cry over you when I finally got to see you," as silent tears dripped onto their joined hands.

"I know, when I was able to think straight I wanted to ask you to come, but everyone kept saying don't try to talk we will catch up later, rest and take one day at a time. But all I wanted was to see you, to reassure you I would be with you as soon as I am home again."

I promised Dr Jo I wouldn't stay too long and would be home in time to help with the small children's bedtime. Ava Blossom has been a great help, for someone who claims to know very little about children she seems very anxious to learn."

Christopher chuckled, "she couldn't have a better teacher than you. Will you come tomorrow? I think I will need lots more kisses to make me better. Miriam blushed, before she could respond Christopher continued, "When I return home will you allow me to see you away from the nursery? Oh I know I join you with the children when you are taking them for an outing. What I am asking is will you join me when you are not on duty. I would enjoy taking you to the theatre, out to dinner and I know you enjoy browsing the museums in Cambridge. In other words Miriam, will you come out with me and share in some of the things we both enjoy, but together."

"You mean as friends, as a close friend?"

"Yes but more than that Miriam, I want us to be more than just friends, but that will have to do for now. When I am fully recovered we will need to talk about us, our hopes and ambitions. After a few seconds a smile lit up Miriam's face, and turning towards the man in the bed whispered, "yes Christopher McKenzie, we will do all of those things as soon as you are better. But I must go now so I will say goodnight and god bless." Leaning over she once again kissed him and turned to leave before she threw caution to the winds and, told him how much she had grown to love him

All the while the two people had been talking, a visitor for Christopher, entered his room. A smile broke out on the face of Great Aunt Grace, who said it was a waste of time praying for something, which on the face of it was impossible? Here before her very eyes was living proof that the power of prayer did work. Her darling youngest great nephew had at long last found his own soul-mate, and he couldn't have made a better choice.

"Christopher, my dear boy it's good to see you awake again and taking notice. Hello Miriam, have you come to kiss Christopher's head and make him better? From where I'm standing it most certainly works. Placing her hand on Christopher's shoulder she leaned over and whispered in his ear, "she is a lovely young woman and you are a very lucky man. Turning to a blushing Miriam said, "Take great care of him, he is still very fragile and will be for the next little while, but all will come right in the end.

Now then young lady may I suggest you use my car to take you back to Church House and my driver can return to take me home later, give Christopher a goodnight kiss, then I will take you to my car and see you on your way. I will return to you Christopher in a trice."

In less than five minutes Dame Grace Drummond returned to the bedside of her nephew. Sitting down she studied his face, she noted the signs of fatigue about his mouth. "Is the pain very bad love? Can I get you anything? Are you taking any painkillers?"

Grace loved all her great nephews and nieces but she had a very special place in her heart for Christopher Sky McKenzie.

When he was about five years old Grace lost the love of her life and one day soon after the funeral she was in the garden at Pipers Gate sitting on a seat shedding a few tears, when a young Christopher came up to her and put his hand into hers saying "would you like me to kiss it better? My Mummy kisses me better when I hurt myself," and before Grace could answer, the small child reached up and kissed her on one cheek and then the other. "Two kisses are better than one, one is to make you better and the other one is because you are sad."

It was at that point Dame Grace Drummond fell in love with this special little boy.

Christopher opened his eyes and looking at his great aunt asked "did you hear what Miriam and I were talking about? When I'm feeling better I will tell you all about it but Miriam is a remarkable lady and I love her so much it hurts."

"Yes love I could see, and from where I was standing I am sure your Miriam returns your love in equal measure. May I sit with you for a short while and perhaps chat about times past? You have been so busy this past couple of years and time goes by so quickly we seem to have lost touch." After a short while Christopher dozed off and Grace was able to greet Kate and Charles Blossom for the first time since Christmas night.

"Hello Aunty Grace it's good to see you, later when it's more convenient perhaps you will explain why you suggested me to play the Good Samaritan in answer to Charles's SOS"

Giving the young couple a quick hug Grace said, "It worked, sorry that is not what I meant to say but I will explain sometime soon." Turning to Christopher again

"I believe your parents are about to come and say goodnight to you so I will leave you for now but hope to see you again tomorrow." Bending over she kissed him saying, "Good night and god bless."

During the drive home Grace allowed herself the luxury of remembering those nine wonderful years when she and her long lost lover John Clayton were reunited, and how a small boy had unknowingly bridged the gap between her terrible grief and the dreadful vacuum her life had become since his death. It was something she would never forget and hoped with all her heart that her boy and his Miriam would experience the same happiness as she had in the autumn days of her life.

CHAPTER 33

"Christina are you sure you feel up to going down for supper?, it's been a gruelling few days for you and under the circumstances I reckon it will do you more good to have a quiet supper up here, just the two of us. Once you have rested we can join the others in time to toast the New Year." As he made his suggestion Sebastian crossed the room and lifting his wife onto his lap cuddled her to him.

"I've missed our cuddle after the boys are settled for the night, something always happened to interrupt us this last few days.

"Sebastian settled back in the chair and placing his hand gently on his wife's tummy asked "how is number three McKenzie doing? I've noticed the morning sickness has stopped, but you must start taking things a bit easier, I will take over the bedtime stint. No, I didn't mean you to be left out, but no lifting the boys out of the bath, they growing heavier by the day."

"Its' not surprising" Christina replied with a chuckle; "they eat like mini horses."

Sebastian snorted with laughter. "Alistair informed me this morning he would like two breakfasts every time."

"Where did that idea come?"

"I'm not altogether sure but it could have been the elder Brice child. He called in this morning while we were just finishing our breakfast and asked if no one wanted the last couple of slices of toast would anybody mind if he ate them. His mother was so embarrassed but not master Brice, he drew up a chair, found a plate and helping himself to the remaining pieces of toast, proceeded to eat them. In order to prevent an ear bashing by his mother he informed us everybody knew growing boys could easily eat two breakfasts."

"So our pair picked up on "growing boys and two breakfasts" laughed their mother.

"Sebastian in answer to your first question, yes I would like just you and me for supper, and providing no one minds I will join in the New Year celebrations in my nightie and housecoat."

"Somehow I don't think you will be the only one ready for bed at the close of 1998, I am sure Patrick is proposing the same to his Lucy.

You know they kept Lucy's pregnancy a secret for almost three months because she was afraid in case something bad happened to the baby. Patrick is almost sure this is due to what happened to her in the past."

"I quite agree with you Sebastian, although she looks fine and acts all serene, no one who really knows her can possibly expect her to be fully over all the trauma of the past few years. She told me once she really believes Patrick saved her from a serious breakdown, his love and compassion touched her very soul. When she said that I must admit I cried."

Dropping a quick kiss on his wife's forehead Sebastian transferred her from his lap into the chair.

"I will go down and collect our supper; Mrs Brice has enough to do this evening."

Sebastian was correct in his assumption regarding Patrick and Lucy. At that precise moment Patrick had just negotiated getting himself and a laden tray with a delicious assortment of supper titbits through the bedroom door without tipping the lot on the floor.

Giving him a beaming smile, Lucy hastily held open the door saying; "My goodness that was a near thing, one more wobble and it would have been all over bar the shouting. It's jolly good job I am still in the early stages of pregnancy, a few more months on and I reckon I wouldn't have been able to move so quickly."

"Can't wait." he answered with a grin.

"Wait for what?"

Putting the tray on a convenient table Patrick came up behind her and wrapping his arms around her placed his hands on her tummy. "Seeing our child growing inside you, feeling as he/she moves, waiting for the time to come into our world, to be part of our family. Surely there can be no greater gift we can receive from each other than to create a small life to nurture and cherish."

Leaning back into her husband's embrace Lucy placed her hands on top of his.

"I love you Patrick McKenzie you are such a good man and I know you will make a good father." she replied as, she groped for her handkerchief

"Sweetheart I didn't mean to make you cry."

"I'm not really crying it's my hormones giving themselves a treat."

"Right back to the business in hand, Mrs Brice has done us a selection of savoury titbits together with a couple of fresh made mince pies and if we would like some pudding she has plenty of both hot and cold. And if we are planning to join the others to see in the New Year I was to let you know the other Mums will be in Nighties and Housecoats/Dressing gowns, the men / daddies smart casual. It was Aubrey who originally suggested the Nighties etc. He agreed with Sebastian the ladies have had a hard time this last few days especially the mums to be, so rather than having to dress up why not come as they are i.e. ready for bed."

"Well we both know more than most how sensitive to any situation our brother- in- law is. So my darling we go as we are," responded Lucy

When Aubrey recounted the response to his suggestion for the ladies to celebrate the New Year in their Nighties etc. his Josephine's reaction was exactly how he imagined.

"You darling clever man, no wonder I love you to bits, this will mean those of us who are not in an interesting condition can indulge in at least one glass of Champagne, of course this can be remedied afterwards." Josephine moved out of her husband's reach as she made this last throw away remark but not fast enough.

"Just what are you suggesting, you wicked woman?" Pulling her down onto his lap he kissed her as though it was going out of fashion.

"Are you feeling broody my love?" Aubrey asked with a catch in his voice.

Some years ago when he and Josephine were first engaged to marry they had each expressed a desire to have more than one child fairly close together, especially as Aubrey was in his words heading towards middle age and wanted to enjoy his children for as many years as he possibly could. Josephine had agreed although she had said at the time it would also be a testament of their deep abiding love for each other.

"Darling, Freddie is now seventeen months old, which will make Oliver three and a bit and Freddie about two and a half. That is if I conceive almost immediately and there is no guarantee I will again quite so quickly." his wife replied with a smile. "Besides think of all the fun we will have trying."

"Come here you temptress, have I told you lately how very much I love you?" Suiting action to words Aubrey proceeded to show his lady just how much he loved and wanted her.

So it was to an unusually quiet house Kate and Charles returned, although lights showed from several of the upper windows, it was the large Christmas tree in the hall, which together with a subdued light, showing from the Drawing room which welcomed the latest arrivals.

"Hello! Is anybody home?"

Heather was just about to come downstairs when she heard Kate call.

"Oh love where have you been? Your mother has been worried sick about you; she hasn't been home very long. After leaving Addenbrooks she and Daniel went straight Pipers Gate to collect some fresh clothes and things before coming back here. So far as I know she and Daniel are having supper in their room and will join the family in time to see the New Year in. Then after checking all is well with Christopher will go to bed for the first time in days and get a good night's sleep." As she finished speaking she gathered the last of her chicks to her and cuddled her in close.

Putting his arms round his beloved Kate, Professor Charles Blossom smiled at the woman still holding Kate's free hand.

"We have just returned from seeing Great Aunt Grace, we found her sitting with Christopher telling him about how she remembered him as a little boy. There she sat holding his hand, reminding him of his earlier escapades and was delighted by his response. After a little while he joined in and told her some of the adventures she hadn't known about. It was at that point our Great Aunt's strategy paid off, one Christopher McKenzie was back with us."

"His memory is back and all he has to do now is to take his time to recuperate, and all being well should be allowed home within the next few days." continued Kate before bursting into tears.

Before Heather could comment further Elizabeth came downstairs followed by Daniel.

"We heard you call out as you arrived what has happened?

Before either Kate or Charles could reply Daniel put his arms round his wife and drawing her close said; "Don't get upset love, let Kate tell us."

Addressing his remarks to his future son-in-law continued, "when we left Christopher a couple of hours ago he was sleeping normally, and his consultant told us all he needs now is plenty of rest to fully recuperate ,although we passed Aunt Grace on her way out so I would hope his doctor hadn't allowed her stay too long."

"That is what we saying to Heather, no, not letting her stay too long, it was the other way about. Kate and I found Great Aunt Grace and your youngest son entertaining each other, with tales of all our yesterdays."

"There was Christopher, sitting up in bed holding on to our Great Aunt's hand and although looking a little worse for wear, chatting to his great aunt."

"Apart from his head wound, still swathed in a dressing, sounding more or less like his old self." chipped in Kate

It was at this point Kate's face seemed to crumble again. "Oh Ma if Christopher hadn't recovered I would have spent the rest of my life blaming myself for asking him to turn on the heating for Charles sister."

Daniel hastened to his step-daughter's side, and putting his arms round her held her close.

"Now then Kate don't beat yourself up any more. What happened was purely accidental, no matter who had gone round to see to the thermostat that morning would most probably have had a nasty headache. As I said it was purely accidental."

"If anyone is to blame it's my fool sister." Charles responded darkly.

"Perhaps next time she might just take the time to advise her family of her change of holiday arrangements."

"Before we close the door on Addenbrooks, what is the latest news about your brother Keith? With all the recent drama within the McKenzie family he seems to have been put on the back burner."

"Lauren's parents returned from Scotland yesterday and have all moved into my house pro-term to look after their daughter and offspring. Until the recent run of tests on Keith is complete everything else is on hold. However in the meantime my parents have invited me to stay with them until the housing is sorted out. They have cut their cruise short and should be back in the U.K sometime tomorrow."

"I have a better idea, now that we know Christopher is out of any immediate danger, why you don't stay with Kate at Pipers Gate after the New Year until your wedding," Elizabeth smiled as she viewed the expression on the face of her daughter.

"It's only a month away. Besides, next year looks as though it's going to be bumper year for surprises."

CHAPTER 34

New Year's morning, this first day of January 1999, was welcomed in a quiet and slightly subdued manner by the residents of Church House. Under normal circumstances the celebrations would have carried on until the wee small hours, but this year all the members of the extended McKenzie family were still coming to terms with the news that Christopher had regained consciousness and was expected in the fullness of time make a complete recovery.

Daniel made the first toast of the New Year at the request of his wife. Taking a glass of Champagne in his hand, then taking Elizabeth's hand in the other hand, joined both their hands around the stem of the glass. Then holding their joint hands high; "To our family may we all rejoice in the news, which we devoutly hope is the full recovery of our son and your brother Christopher. We have dealt with the fear and uncertainty over his injuries, but never lost the faith. Get well soon my son." Daniels voice broke as he toasted the young man whom he regarded as his son.

"To Christopher, may he continue to progress towards a full recovery."

It was then Sebastian who proposed a toast to the full extended McKenzie family.

"First to existing McKenzie's, the soon to become family members, and the yet to be born McKenzie's, Happy New Year 1999 is going to be a great year for all of us."

Sebastian was later to confess to his wife he couldn't have said another word if he had been offered £1000. The relief he felt when Addenbrooks had told them his kid brother was going to get better had made him realise how much he loved him.

"I'm sure the rest of us felt the same." replied Christina. "I was watching Kate and Charles Blossom, the joy and relief, on their faces was almost overwhelming."

"I know sweetheart, but we can now start looking forward to what is going to be a momentous new year."

Later, on this first day of January 1999, Aubrey suggested to his brothers-in-law they had a meeting later in the day, preferably just the three of them in his study, when the small fry where having their afternoon nap.

"I happen to know the Mums usually have a rest about the same time so this will not eat into what Josephine and me call our quality time. Daniel is going to take Ma to Addenbrooks and I will bring him into the loop later on."

Patrick and Sebastian nodded in agreement. So the first step was been taken in what was to become a bizarre situation.

Just before the family were summoned to take their places for the special New Year's Day lunch an old fashioned Rolls Royce drew smoothly to a stop outside the front door of Church House. The sound of the big brass knocker being rapped hard twice echoed round the main entrance hall.

"Who in the world." but before Patrick had time to finish his question the majestic figure of his Great Aunty Grace swept in towards assemble family and guests.

Making a bee-line for her niece, she handed her a large bouquet of very early spring flowers, and a very large bottle of brandy to Daniel

"Happy New Year to you both and may all of you have a very Happy, Peaceful and Prosperous New Year., I would very much like to join you all for the now famous New Years Day dinner, which I know you hold at one o'clock sharp on this, the first day of the year. I also want to join in celebrating my Great Nephew's recovery. You must know how important this family is to me."

Within seconds an extra place was laid for this totally unexpected guest but made very welcome nonetheless.

During the meal the conversation ranged over a wide range of topics but the two primary subjects were Christopher's continued care, and the forthcoming wedding between Kate and her Professor.

The three senior adults present, Elizabeth, Daniel and Heather were adamant Christopher would be better off staying at the family home in Suffolk while Aubrey and Josephine would have preferred he stay at Church House, but agreed Pipers Gate would be a tad more peaceful. Having got that thorny subject sorted out to everybody's satisfaction, they turned their collective attention to the forthcoming wedding.

Addressing his questions to the happy couple Daniel inquired if they had decided upon a particular date and place.

Small mundane matters such as the reception, where Charles and Kate would live etc. and of course all the paraphernalia required by the bride and bridegroom to be.

"Its' going to take a bit of organising but if you feel you can trust me to take care of most of the planning for the actual day I will be delighted help in any way I can." Daniel beamed as he waited for their comments.

"Daniel your generosity in offering to take on what I would call this monumental undertaking at such short notice leaves me almost speechless."

Before Charles could continue Kate started to laugh.

"My darling man this must be the first time ever, but Step-Papa, I second what Charles has said and will gladly hand over all the arrangements to your more than capable self. However I think under the circumstances it will be better if the female contingent of the family take the responsibility for the personal bits and bobs required by the bride, that's me" she finished with a mile wide smile.

"However before we can make any further plans I must check with my sister-in-law to see if she has had any further news of my brother Keith."

Elizabeth looked appalled. "Charles I am so very sorry, with all that's happened during the last few days I have never asked once of your brother's condition. You must be worried sick and, yet never once let on so not as to upset Kate. We, that is Daniel and I, are going to Addenbrooks shortly, would you and Kate care to come with us or would you prefer to go on your own? Oh lord I'm making a mess of this, what I mean you together with Kate in your own car, which makes sense, you can come home as and when you wish. At this stage I'm not sure how long we will stay with Christopher, it all depends on how he is. I do know his consultant has stressed he is to rest as much as possible. How my boy will manage this I cannot say at this stage, but knowing my son, rest will be the last thing on his agenda."

As soon as the meal over those bound for the hospital prepared to leave. Michael and Fiona Shaw asked Daniel if they could join them. "We want to see for ourselves Christopher is making progress, beside when he comes home we will have some ideas as to how to keep him entertained," Michael said trying hard but not quite succeeding in keeping a straight face," and of course making sure he has plenty of rest " added Fiona with an almost pious smile. Daniel gave the two young people soon to become McKenzie's, a look as though to say who do you think you are kidding. "Yes I think a visit from you two would be a very good idea, but remember, quiet and stress free."

Great Aunty Grace elected to return to Long Melford and was expecting her chauffeur in about forty minutes or so. This just left Heather who had taken the unusual step of asking Charles to drop her of at his house in Sycamore Road as she wanted to check up on Lauren and baby Hugo Charles.

No one commented but more than one person wondered what it was that attracted Heather to this little family. Had Christopher been there he could have explained the what-fore, why and how's, but he wasn't so the matter was put on the back burner for the time-being.

CHAPTER 35

At a few minutes after four o'clock just as the sun was making up its mind to get ready for bed, the sky was tinged with pink turning to a delicate shade of pale mauve which in the space of just a few more minutes would once again change to almost indigo. The first stars of the evening were showing as Aubrey ushered his two brothers-in-law into his study. Each husband and father had taken time to explain to their wives what had taken place in relation to the surprise visit of Dr and Mrs Walsh. They had also explained the reasoning behind the meeting between the three men to take place while the children were having a rest.

Patrick had very gently asked Lucy did she wish to meet her Aunt Rosalie, but Lucy had very wisely suggested it would be better if Patrick did not include her until he was certain it would be in her best interest.

"It's very thoughtful of you ask Patrick but I am more than happy be guided by you. Somehow like you and the others, I think these people have a hidden agenda but I have a greater worry, how is this meeting going to affect Aubrey and Dr. Jo?"

However Aubrey had already spoken about this with both Sebastian and Patrick but more importantly with his beloved Josephine. Holding her close with his arms wrapped around her, he told her what he said when her eldest brother had asked him what his feelings were towards Rosalie Forsythe turning up out of the blue.

"Josephine, my Josephine, that day you said yes to my proposal I told you I loved you more than life itself. I promised to love you each and every day until the end of time. Now if it were humanly possible I love you more than ever. You are my Love, my Life, and my very beloved Wife."

Putting her gently away from him he departed at once because he knew, if he stayed just one more second he would have said to hell with them at least wait five days giving them, the Walsh's time to return to South Africa.

Sebastian had explained to Christina as they lay in bed the night before. Holding her close he told her of the extraordinary couple who seemed hell bent in causing trouble for the McKenzie's and Aubrey-Page

"Don't allow them to rattle you sweetheart, keep your cool and let them do the talking. I happen to know you are very good at that, but this is very close to home. Patrick will handle them especially as his Lucy is carrying their baby."

"You are so right as usual my love, how come I am so lucky to be married to loveliest lady in the land? But I will promise you this; no one and I mean nobody will ever be allowed to threaten those who I hold most dear to me.

You and our boys and any other children we are blessed with are more precious than a king's ransom. Now let's talk about something much nicer than these very unwelcome visitors."

"So gentlemen please make yourselves comfortable and when you are ready Sebastian will you kick off?"

So without further delay Sebastian related what had taken place five days ago. After he finished his narrative he waited for his companions to comment.

Aubrey was first to speak.

"I have discussed these totally unexpected turn of events with Josephine a little while ago. The reason I didn't talk to her earlier was because I did not want to allow these people to spoil our family Christmas. I have also told her of your question Sebastian, how do I feel about Rosalie Forsythe coming back into my life after all these years? I have re-assured my wife she has nothing whatsoever to fear. I love my Josephine and will continue to do so until the end of time.

However, I have a suspicious mind and I do not believe for one moment that these people are looking Lucy up for either Rosalie's brother sake or because she feels the need to make sure her long lost niece is in safe hands. Something is not quite kosher."

Patrick raised his hand; "I would like to suggest we look at this from another angle. Is it feasible they are actually trying to locate Michael and Fiona Shaw and are using Lucy as away in?"

Patrick allowed his words to sink in then continued. "We know that their father pleaded guilty to both charges 1. To supplying false documents for the assistance of illegal immigrants into this country. 2. Perverting the course of Justice. Because of the guilty plea there was no need for a jury, and due to the serious nature of both crimes he is at present serving a sentence of six years for the first crime and five for the second with a parole hearing after six years."

It was at this point Aubrey interrupted." He should have been given ten years for what he did to his children especially our lovely gentle Lucy."

For a moment no one spoke.

"I quite agree with you but at the same time I am at a loss to understand what they hope to achieve." responded Sebastian.

"What day did you arrange to meet up with them?" queried Patrick.

"I suggested I visited them in their hotel on a date to be arranged. I explained I would not be returning to London until the 4th of January soonest, but if Christina is still feeling unwell I may just stay a while longer either here or go back to Pipers Gate."

"May I make a suggestion? Why not remain here for a few more days, leaving one of us to contact Dr and Mrs Walsh inviting them to Bedford Square on the 4th of January for say, a meeting immediately after lunch. This should give you time to have one of your special branch friends have a look-see into their background, while Patrick can do a little checking up on Dr Walsh.

See where he trained, where he has been, and doing what, with whom over the last few years." As Aubrey finished speaking Sebastian nodded his head in agreement.

"So we all travel to London first thing on the morning of the 4th I will get Jim Harris to contact Dr Walsh and his wife for a meeting with us as suggested.

It will also be a good idea to have Jim to make the arrangements which will mean they will not know exactly who will be present when they arrive. So gentlemen, let us leave is for now, then first thing tomorrow I will contact my special branch friend and leave you two to start digging on Dr Walsh."

As the three men rose to leave they became aware of a slight but definite commotion coming from the direction of the front-door.

"Carefully does it, no leave the chair to me love, we can manage; there you are now nearly there."

Aubrey reached the door in almost one single stride and the first person he saw was the back of his Step-Papa Daniel, which very effectively blocked out the view of the outer-hall entrance. Then the quiet voice of the very last person they expected to see on this late afternoon of this cold and frosty New Year's Day.

"I'm fine Ma, don't fret now, just let your husband do it his way he has managed very well up to now. Come on love, there is no need to cry everything is going to be alright."

"Christopher; Christopher; Thank God." Three voices, all with a different greeting but the look of joy on their faces said it all.

CHAPTER 36

Christopher McKenzie was back with his family, looking decidedly better than the last time his sisters had seen him.

Josephine had been pre-warned by a telephone call from her mother more or less just about the time the three remaining men had gone into Aubrey's study. Deciding not to interrupt she had wisely played down the news her youngest brother was being discharged from hospital into the collective care of his family.

With the help of Mr and Mrs Brice she had managed in the time allotted to transform one of their reception rooms into a cosy bed-sit for the semi invalid. Although Christopher protested at being termed a semi anything, by the time he was settled into bed he was very glad to rest.

After reassuring everybody he was not in any danger of a relapse it was unanimously agreed he could have visitors but just a few at a time.

"You will know love when you are ready to become completely involved with the whole family in one hit. So just be patient for a little while longer and let nature take its course." Josephine kissed her brother and after giving him a gentle hug went to explain to her husband and two older brothers what had transpired during their meeting.

"Dr. Lewis and his colleagues explained Christopher was no longer in danger but would need a period of rest and observation for the next seven to fourteen days. Normally he would be transferred from intensive care into a unit where his condition would be monitored in a more relaxed environment," Elizabeth explained. "But Daniel asked if there was any reason why our son couldn't do this at home."

Daniel squeezed her hand and taking up the tale continued. "Dr Lewis suggested we, that is your Ma and me go and have a cup of tea while he had a word with the rest of his team. At first I was at a loss to understand, surely we should be present, especially as it would be our joint responsibility to make sure Christopher adhered to any necessary treatment to enable him to make a complete recovery.

However after the doctor explained he wanted to make a full examination of his patient, in order to make absolutely sure he was well enough to undertake the short journey to Church House. I think your Ma was surprised as I was. We had naturally thought we would be going straight to Pipers Gate. But no, it had to be here; of course it made perfect sense. First Christopher has a resident doctor on hand, and secondly he will be just five to ten minutes away from Addenbrooks if he has to be re-admitted in an emergency."

Taking a deep breath Daniel continued. "So once the rest of the team had their say we telephoned Josephine to clear it with her and Aubrey, and bless her she explained you were having a meeting with Sebastian and Patrick but insisted there is no problem. So here we are all three of us."

Daniel looked at the assembled members of his adopted family and taking a large handkerchief blew his nose hard.

"When we told Kate and Charles our news Charles said he would drive directly to Sycamore Road to pick up Heather and bring her straight back here. He wouldn't tell her why but knew she would be very hurt to *miss her boy's homecoming.*

In fact I do believe they have just arrived. Let me go and open the door." Elizabeth crossed the hall towards the door.

The next few minutes were slightly chaotic but very soon order was restored thus leaving Heather to see for herself one of her yew lambs had been returned to the fold safe, if not fully well.

Folding whom she secretly considered her boy into her arms she carefully held him away from her embrace.

"Oh you have no idea how pleased I am to have you home. I won't pester you with questions; all that matters is you are safe. All you have to do is get fit and well again, but that will come in time. I promised myself I wouldn't cry over you but I don't think I can keep that promise." she said as she wiped her face with the back of her hand.

"Here use this love, nobody but you and me will know." as he said this Christopher put the edge of the sheet into Heather's hand. "I won't tell if you don't. Come on now there is no reason to cry anymore I am home and as you say, all I have to do is get better."

Giving Heather a sideways look asked "do you still play a killer game of Scrabble?" As Heather nodded her head he continued. "Right Mrs Wilson, give me a couple of days then we plan a match, in the meantime any chance of cuppa and perhaps a slice of Christmas cake?"

As Heather turned to leave Christopher called her back."Heather will you do something very special for me? Will you ask Miriam to come and say goodnight. I don't know if anyone has told her I'm home and she will be so hurt to find out without being told."

Coming back to his bedside Heather looked down at her boy with a wealth of understanding. "I'm so pleased for you if I think what you are trying to say, does she know how you feel about her? I won't ask any more questions for now, but I'll make sure no one comes in here while you say goodnight to your Miriam."

Heather found Miriam just as she was going into her bedroom." Miriam I have some good news for you, Christopher is home and has asked me to tell you and to show you where he is at present. He also asked if you will please go down and give him a bedtime kiss."

Miriam for a few seconds stood perfectly motionless, then with a strangled sob put her hands over her face and just stood there in front of Heather, unable to control her tears.

"Heather I'm so sorry to cry like a water spout but I have been so afraid, not of Christopher but what the family will think. My background is different, I am classed as Eurasian. This means one parent was White English and the other Asian.

In my case my mother was from Solihull and my father was high cast Indian. They both met while studying at Oxford University. But that was a long time ago. I will just make sure Dr Jo knows where I am in case she needs me, perhaps you will then take me to where Christopher is." Giving Heather a tentative smile she went along to Josephine's suit before going with Heather towards Christopher's designated bedsit.

CHAPTER 37

It wasn't until after the evening meal was over the family came together in what is known as Aubrey's Parlour. Under normal circumstances this room was for the Page family's personal use only. But on this the first night of 1999 Aubrey suggested everyone would be welcome to join him and Josephine.

"Elizabeth and Daniel will be along presently they are making sure Christopher is settled." As he spoke they both entered the room closing the door quietly behind them.

"Christopher is going to have a sleep for now but hopes to wish you all good night before you go to bed."

"He's not going to get up and come in here is he?"

"No Kate he has more sense than to expect he can pick up as he left off, but I did suggest that each couple said their own good-night before retiring. Just to re-assure yourselves he is on the road to recovery, not a question and answer session." Daniel smiled as he spoke to take any implied sting out of his words.

Later when Josephine and Aubrey were getting ready for bed Aubrey brought up the result of his discussion with her two older brothers, in relation to the strange affair with Dr and Mrs Walsh.

"Sebastian is going to speak to Jim Harris in the morning then all we can do is to play it by ear. Hopefully before many more days have passed we will know some of the answers, if not all of them.

However no matter what is said or implied Josephine, you are my one and only love, now and forever. You are never to doubt my feelings for you."

It was at this point Josephine remembered Miriam's response to Christopher's habitual over indulgence in having two large teaspoonfuls of sugar in his tea or coffee.

"Aubrey, earlier yesterday Miriam came to ask permission if she might visit Christopher at Addenbrooks. I asked her how she would get there, I suggested she could possibly go with Kate and Ava but she very politely declined and said she would go another time. As she turned to leave, I noticed how upset she was; no she didn't say anything it was the expression on her face. Sorry love, I'm not making sense, she looked how I felt the time before Patrick's wedding, when you thought you wouldn't get to Pipers Gate before 13th. Do you think Miriam and my brother are attracted to one another?"

"I'm not sure, but I do know his attention became decidedly cooler towards Sybil Buchannan about the time of Freddie's first birthday, and not long afterwards he seemed to spend an unusual amount of time with our children. I have met him more than once with Miriam taking our pair out for a walk. Oliver certainly enjoyed his Uncle Christopher's attention, he Oliver, usually ended up riding on his uncle's shoulders."

"Do you think there is an attraction between them?"

"I honestly don't know, but I wouldn't be surprised, Miriam is a very lovely young woman, both to look at and more importantly, she has a kind and caring nature. I can testify to the latter. If I tell you how I know, I must have your solemn promise to keep secret what I am about to tell you. Josephine I am not questioning your integrity, but this is Miriam's story and how I became involved with her."

"Aubrey, I know you, and I do understand your reason for asking for my promise. Of course I willingly give it, but are you quite sure you want me to know?"

"Yes, I think in this instance it is important, because if what I suspect is correct, it will remove any reason why this couple should not develop their feelings into a mutual and loving relationship."

Drawing his wife into his arms he held her close.

"I will give you a brief outline of Miriam's maternal back ground. Her mother was the second daughter of Harold and Sharon Davidson. Sharon's parents could be termed to be epitome of respectability. Her father was the manager of the local bank, while her mother the pillar of the Towns Women's Gild, plus several charitable organisations.

Sharon's elder daughter, Joanne after leaving school worked in the local library and, in due course married an equally respectable young man with prospects.

Of course the youngest daughter Sarah was expected to follow the family line, but not this girl, she set her sights on going to university, but not any old university, it had to be Oxford, nothing else would do.

At first her father laughed, who did she think she was, only the best could obtain a place there, then the vexed question of who would pay for her grandiose ideas. Why couldn't she be content, get a job like her sister, besides she would get married and then what good would her education be.

"Josephine that is how it was in those early post war days; keep your head down, keep going and hope for better days.

Sarah was determined to achieve her goal, she worked hard at school and eventually went up to Oxford to read international finance and economics. Needless to say her father was forever boasting about his clever daughter and how well she was doing, no mention of his opposition to her going in the first place.

Sarah met and fell in love with a third year student reading Law and Politics. However the young man was a high cast Indian, whose parents managed one of the largest tea plantations in the tea plantation area of the Sub Continent, and after the partition of India his father became the largest share holder in the company. Sarah took her fiancé back to Solihull to meet her parents.

Mega shock, her father rages, shouting you are marrying someone like that, you are no daughter of mine and her mother indulged in a fit of hysterics. The outcome was daughter leaves parental home vowing never to darken their doors again.

Sarah and Michael Kahn marry and set up home in leafy Letchworth Garden City, where they had one child a daughter Miriam in 1974.

The young couple worked hard and could afford to send their only child to a very good public school for girls. They took holidays overseas, and on several occasions spent summer vacations in India with Michael's family. The Kahn's made Sarah welcome but were never quite sure if or when the time came would Michael and his family be prepared to settle on the plantation in India. Unfortunately the question did not arise. In 1986 Michael was killed in a freak accident leaving a widow and his twelve year old daughter Miriam.

Sharon's Indian in- laws wanted her to go to them in India, but this would mean Miriam becoming a boarder at her school and Sharon felt her daughter had already lost one parent, so to leave her in England would be much too stressful for the child," pausing to have a drink of water Aubrey carried on.

"Sarah's parents decided it would be better if Sarah and child stayed with them until she found her feet again, so the die was cast for a tragedy that would have appalling consequences.

Sarah returned to Solihull the family home of her childhood and gradually joined in the social side of life, but there was still a void left by Michael's death, until one evening Harold Davidson brought a young presentable man to dinner.

Introducing him to Sarah saying, "This is Gerald Howard the youngest chairman of the Chamber of Commerce, this man is going places mark my words, at the same time listing Sarah's scholastic achievements. Sarah was to remark to her mother later, "Father sounded as though he was offering me for sale."

Gerald Howard became a regular visitor and always made a point being there when Sarah was at home. Of course her parents made him welcome, insisting it was in Sarah's best interest to remarry, and Miriam needed a father figure in her life.

The usual claptrap some parents inflict on the children. In 1990 Sarah finally gave in and married Gerald Howard. Six months later Miriam's nightmare began. Little things at first, Gerald's arm thrown around her shoulders, just casually brush the side of her young developing breasts or dropping a kiss on her cheek while giving her a squeeze.

She complained to her mother and asked her to make him stop, but mother said he was only trying to be affectionate. But Sarah did speak to her husband and his response was to backhand her across her face for daring to suggest he would do such a thing, besides Miriam had quite a way to go before his thoughts would turn in that direction. Sarah had never in all her life had anyone strike her in that manner. The next day Gerald took her in his arms and said he was so sorry but the idea she really thought he could do what her little bitch of a daughter was suggesting made him furiously angry. He promised it wouldn't ever happen again. His promise and all sub sequent promises were worthless and his sexual harassment of Miriam was becoming bolder, until one night he went one step too far. Miriam was cutting out some material into assorted pieces; she was making a patchwork quilt when Gerald came into her room without knocking. It was obvious he had been drinking, and grabbing his step daughter round the waist informed her in the crudest terms what he was going to do to her. Miriam screamed at him to let her go, and kept on screaming as he struggled to drag her to the bed. In desperation the terrified young woman drove the dressmaking scissors deep into his abdomen.

In the ensuring commotion of police, ambulance, hysterical mother and terrified girl it was almost impossible to get a coherent story of what actually happened.

It wasn't until some five days later Gerald Howard made a charge against his stepdaughter of grievous bodily harm, with intent to murder.

Despite Miriam protesting her innocence, she ended up in court facing these charges.

I was not the presiding judge for the case, and the girl in the dock was facing a lengthy term in prison if she was found guilty. However, one of my colleagues also took an interest but for an entirely different reason.

The same man Gerald Howard had been charged with sexual assault about twelve years ago, but the charge was withdrawn. There had been talk of a large payment of money changing hands, but nothing was proved.

In the course of the trial, the defence pulled a rabbit out of the hat. One of Miriam's friends produced a couple of Miriam's diaries for the last two years. Miriam had placed them in her safe keeping because she was sure someone had been going through her possessions in her room. Questioned why had these diaries not been produced before this late date, the parent of the young person who had the diaries explained the family had been in Australia for six weeks and had only returned to the UK some twenty-four hours ago.

The prosecution barristers protested and requested the diaries should not be submitted, but the defence claimed they could prove the Gerald Howard was lying through his teeth.

In view of the seriousness of the charges the presiding judge called for a recess and invited both sets of barristers into his rooms together with the disputed diaries.

After taking time to read the diary entries he informed the barristers, in view of the serious charges Miss Kahn was facing in his opinion the diaries had to be presented as evidence.

In the fullness of time the situation was reversed Miriam Kahn was acquitted and Mr Gerald Howard was arrested where he was charged with several cases of sexual intimidation, rape of a minor, attempted rape of several underage girls, and grievous bodily harm against Miriam Kahn and his wife Mrs Sarah Howard.

I was the presiding judge, and if I tell you the creature in the dock was one of the most depraved, sadistic pieces of worthless humanity I have ever had the misfortune to meet."

Josephine had never seen such a look of loathing on her husband's face, "what happened to him?

"Thirty five years and a directive to serve twenty eight years before he can apply for parole, with the proviso he would be placed on the sex offenders register and had to report to his probation officer on a weekly basis."

CHAPTER 38

Early on the morning of January 4th 1999 the two elder McKenzie men together with Aubrey, Daniel, and Michael Shaw departed for London. Jim Harris had confirmed he had arranged a meeting with the Walsh's for three pm on the same day. This would take place at the business premises of McKenzie S.I. 27 Bedford Square.

"I didn't tell them who they would be meeting with. Although the female, who claims to be Mrs Patrick's aunt asked if 'little Lindsay would be there, she just couldn't wait to meet her again. I should take that with a pinch of salt if it was me."

The tone of Jim's voice left Sebastian in no doubt his opinion of Dr Walsh and his wife.

The five men arrived in London in time to avail themselves of the hot soup and an array of sandwiches provided by the resident house-keeper.

Immediately lunch was over it was decided Michael would stay in Patrick's apartment, Jim Harris would bring the Walsh's into the interview room adjacent to Sebastian's office, making sure the intercom was switched on.

"This will enable you both to hear what is going on. I think Patrick and I should meet them first. This is initially to ascertain exactly what they are after but if they start to waffle on I will have to bring in the big guns, that's you two." as he said this Sebastian gave a wolfish grin.

"That's fine by me." replied Daniel.

"I would prefer to keep a low profile, but if at any point Mrs Walsh puts one foot out of line you can count on my support." as he spoke

Aubrey-Page felt a surge of adrenalin ,nothing and no-one was allowed to threaten his extended family. And he would be damned if someone from his very distant past is going to try for a game of happy families.

Patrick's thoughts were on a similar line. If this woman who claims to be Lucy's aunt was genuine, she had some serious explaining to do. He recalled something his Ma had said when his bothers had been trying to find who was responsible for beating his darling wife almost to death. Who had seen the photographs of her before and after the event? His mother had asked this all important question, but up to now had remained unanswered.

One question had led to another, Patrick was known for his patience, especially in a situation such as this and, knew until he had all the known facts he would not commit himself to putting into words his suspicions.

Having a fair idea what was going through his brother's mind Sebastian placed his hand on Patrick's arm.

"Let us hear what this pair is after, then, if necessary we will bring in the other two. One way or the other this starts and finishes today."

The doorbell rang while at the same time someone banged the knocker loudly three times.

Jim took his time in answering the door. "Let them sweat a bit," he muttered to himself.

Opening the door to these people who he felt were nothing but trouble invited them to follow him. Opening the conference room door he announced in a sonorous tone. "Dr and Mrs Walsh Sir." standing back he ushered the couple in.

Sebastian rose to greet them but Patrick remained seated.

"Good after noon, I am Sebastian McKenzie and this is my brother Patrick.

Please take a seat," indicating two chairs either side of a coffee table he continued. "When you came to Pipers Gate last week you didn't say exactly why or give a reason for your visit. We have arranged this meeting at no little inconvenience to ourselves, so if you will please state your business with McKenzie S.I.

Before we commence I suggest it will be in all our interests to have this meeting recorded." Placing a small rectangular box in the middle of the coffee table Sebastian nodded towards Dr Walsh inviting him to begin.

Patrick was to tell Lucy later it was Sebastian at his best.

"I am Doctor Peter Walsh and this is my wife Rosalie. We are here at the request of Mr Aidan Forsythe, as you are aware he is at present in America, allegedly being involved with some kind of art fraud. He asked if we should find ourselves in London would we call and check on his daughter to ensure all was well with her."

Peter Walsh looked across at his wife expecting her to pick up where he left off, but she just sat there looking blank, as Sebastian was to report to Christina later.

The silence was deafening, neither of the McKenzie men spoke, it was an old ploy they hadn't invited the Walsh's in the first instance. It was very obvious they wanted something, so let them make the first move.

After what seemed to be a long pause it was Rosalie Walsh who finally broke the silence.

"I haven't seen my niece since she was a very small child and despite what you might think of my long absence from these shores. I feel it only right and proper to correct this situation, especially as her father is very anxious to know if all is well with her. I together with my husband would very much like to spend some time with her before returning to South Africa later this month."

"Of course we would like to meet up with her extended family, we understand she has two half siblings a boy and a girl. The last we heard about them they all lived somewhere in the North East of England." broke in Dr Walsh.

Once again the silence seemed to hang in the air waiting for someone to pick up where Dr Walsh left off.

"It has been a very long time since I last held little Lindsay, it was just before her mother took off and left my poor brother without wife or child." Rosalie dabbed at her eyes with a tissue before continuing. "We all missed her so much."

"How old was Little Lindsay when you last spoke to her?" enquired Patrick in quiet voice.

"Just after her second birthday, we had a picnic in the garden as I remember." Rosalie Walsh replied with a half smile. "We had such a lovely day."

"Did you play with the child Mrs Walsh and can you remember if she had any particular favourite toys etc?" Patrick continued to probe.

"Not that I can recall." replied her Aunt "it was a very long time ago."

"Did you take any photographs at the time?" Patrick continued to press for answers.

Rosalie placed a hand under her chin then shook her head. "Sorry I cannot remember perhaps I did but I don't have them now. But I do recall she was or is the spitting image of her daddy, the same lovely dark hair and his lovely eyes, the same blue as a summer sky."

Sebastian caught his brother's eye before Patrick could say another word.

"So Mrs Walsh you haven't seen or spoken to your niece since she was removed from Ireland."

"Unfortunately not, I stayed with my brother for a long time, until he decided to go to study art in Italy, I kept in touch for a while but Aidan seemed to drift off into a world of his own and it was then I decided to get my life back. I had supported him for years but one day I said enough is enough, so although older than the usual student nurse I did my nursing training in Dublin where I met Peter, we married and not long afterwards we both decided we wanted to work in South Africa."

"We have worked there for the past ten years and until very recently we were very content." her husband cut in.

Sebastian picked up on the last part of the Doctor's statement. "What changed, was it the political situation or something more personal?" he asked.

"The former." the doctor responded, the racial tensions were becoming increasingly unbearable. Good friends and colleagues were arrested and held without trial, some disappeared overnight and it was not just a matter of colour but deeply held beliefs. This is one of the reasons we decided to take a break and come back to the U.K.

It was at this point Jim Harris knocked on the interview room door and crossing the room whispered quietly in Sebastian's ear. Giving a nod Sebastian excused himself explaining he would be back presently suggesting they take a break and would arrange to have his housekeeper bring in refreshments in his absence.

CHAPTER 39

Sebastian had barely closed his own office door behind before Aubrey explained the reason for his summons.

"Sebastian that woman is not Rosalie Forsythe; so far as I am aware she never did meet up with or see Lucy as a baby. She couldn't stand Dorothy, and when Rosalie was told Aidan was going to marry her she was furiously angry and most definitely refused to attend the wedding. Rosalie always blamed Dorothy for leading her brother down the path to self destruction. I didn't take that view myself because Aidan always had a wild streak in him and although very gifted, couldn't settle to anything for very long. I suppose the bottom line was once the thrill wore off he lost interest, and of course at the time it was very fashionable to be a rebel."

"Like drinking and drugs." countered Daniel?

"Exactly." replied Aubrey, "plus of course our girl Lucy has the most beautiful hazel eyes and not summer blue like her father."

"Yes both Patrick and I picked up on that, which means she did not see Lucy as a toddler or as you say Aubrey, she is not Rosalie."

"But how do you explain the likeness to Lucy." asked Daniel, "even Jim Harris noticed how alike the person calling herself Rosalie is to Lucy?"

"I suggest we all return and ask her," was Sebastian's reply to Daniels question.

So following Sebastian's suggestion all three men returned to join Patrick and their questionable visitors.

It was difficult to decide who was more surprised as the three men stepped inside the room. Rosalie made no attempt to greet Aubrey as one would expect after such a long period, especially as they had originally been engaged to be married. She barely acknowledged his presence other than a cool nod in his direction and a very quiet Good Afternoon.

Sebastian lost no time in making introductions all round.

"This is my Step-Father Professor Daniel Gibson and brother-in-law Mr Aubrey Page QC. These two gentlemen have both been very much involved with your niece Mrs Walsh in the last three years. My brother Christopher became involved with her much earlier than that. It was he who found her after she had suffered a traumatic beating which left her without memory or speech.

Then again he came to her rescue after being found not guilty on the charge of murdering her mother."

Patrick shot to his feet, "where were you then Mrs Walsh, where was her father, the man who should have been there to help and protect her?"

Daniel laid his hand on Patrick's arm. "Take it easy son; it will all be sorted very soon."

Looking towards the Doctor and his wife Daniel continued, "I don't know who you are but there is one thing both Mr Aubrey Page and I are in absolute agreement is that you Mrs Walsh, although you show a remarkable resemblance to Lucinda are most definitely not Rosalie Forsythe." Holding up his hand to prevent her speaking continued, I have known Patrick's wife since the day she came to my establishment for help, she lost her speech after the beating she received and it was only through the love and devotion she received from the McKenzie family, together with the care and love of her cousin Christina, and lately myself that she regained her voice and trust. And I for one will not permit either you or your husband to cause her one moment of anxiety or fear, therefore on behalf of my sons and son-in-law I sincerely hope I have made our feelings clear on the subject."

Once again there was stony silence.

This time it was broken by a deep sigh from Dr Walsh.

"Gentlemen it is time to clear this whole god dam mess up once and for all.

You are quite correct my wife is not Rosalie Forsythe she is Aiden Forsythe's second cousin Veronica. Aidan's father and Veronica's father were full cousins and both carry the family likeness. Rosalie and Veronica were both trained nurses when I met up with them in Dublin. I fell in love with Rosalie and in the fullness of time we married and after a while settled in South Africa working in a hospital for the poor outside Cape Town. For five wonderful years Rosalie and I worked together, it was hard work but we kept each other going.

I knew about you Mr Aubrey Page, Rosalie explained about your relationship during your younger days, and how every time she wanted to return to England her selfish unprincipled brother threatened suicide, and the only time she actually left he took an overdose and the parish priest managed to get word to her before she left Ireland.

I loved her so much, she was a kind and caring woman, and I really and truly believe she loved my back." Taking a shuddering breath he continued;" Then one day she complained of having a dreadful sick head ache, at first I thought it was something akin to a Flue like virus but after a couple of days she was much worse. But it was not anything like that, it was a malarial type of bug which attacked her immune system and in less than one week my beautiful Rosalie was dead.

When Veronica heard she flew out to Cape Town to offer her condolences, then she stayed on to help in the hospital. Her services were more than welcome, trained nurses are hard to come by especially those who didn't mind caring for the coloured people."

Pausing to rub his hand over his face Peter Walsh continued with his story. "So after a few years Veronica and I married, it was not a love match, it was more for companionship, but we managed to bumble along until in the early hours one morning one of our closest friends and colleagues was arrested without warning, no charges were brought, he simply disappeared.

Naturally we were both very upset, but Veronica said not to worry she knew a way to fix it, all we had to do was try to find a way of locating our friend and getting him released on bail.

I did not ask how she intended to manage this, but all she would say was I had to arrange to have him here in our house as soon as possible and she would take care of the rest. This being papers to get him safely out of South Africa and into the UK."

All eyes turned towards the bogus Rosalie.

"Yes I did what had to done." Veronica spoke up loudly and somewhat defiant. "I remember seeing a photograph of Lindsay Shawcross in one of the British national dailies. It carried the story of a young girl having received such a beating her injuries left her without memory or speech. I remembered Rosalie showing me a photograph of her niece taken shortly after she was born and think I remarked at the time Rosalie could have been her mother they were so much alike. Anyway I recognised the girl, the newspaper report was very detailed and I later remembered that Lindsay's father or step father was into printing. So I made contact with Mrs Shawcross and threatened her with exposure unless she pursued her husband to make a set of papers which would enable our African friend to escape to England. But there is always a price to be paid, and once it became known I knew someone who could procure the necessary documentation to help others to escape I was in over my head.

Then Dorothy sent word she and her husband wanted out, they were going to the police to confess what they had been doing. Mr Shawcross had been visited by some very unpleasant people who wanted him to do various things for them in the same line of work, but not for the same reason as we," here she indicated her husband, "were doing for our friends."

Her husband took up the story. "We made a special visit to the Shawcross household. Mrs Shawcross insisted we visited her after dark; this was during the summer month of July which meant it didn't get really dark until very late. When we arrived we went round to the outer door at the rear of the house as instructed, where we were told there would be no more papers not now not ever. We both pleaded with Mrs Shawcross but she was adamant. Veronica stepped towards her pleading if she couldn't supply any more paperwork would she at least give us five days before going to the police, this would give us time to get back home. But she absolutely refused. Then to our horror Mrs Shawcross picked up a long bladed knife and started to make slashing movements in front of her while at the same time coming closer and closer to Veronica, I stepped in to try and take the knife from her but she reached out and picked up a second one with her left hand. I grabbed her left hand but she was too quick for me, she slashed down at me and missed completely but cut her own arm in several places. I let go of her arm and reached for a tea towel from the table to try and stem the blood but in the meantime she had managed to slash through Veronica's jacket and cut her from the collarbone down the side of her chest almost to her waist. There was blood everywhere. In the struggle that followed Mrs Shawcross was cut several times as I tried to wrest the knives from her. It was during that dreadful struggle that the tip of the long knife caught the side of her throat. Unfortunately it was an artery in her neck which was cut causing her death. It was a dreadful accident, but because of the circumstances prior to her death we knew the police would never believe her death was just a dreadful accident."

Dr Peter Walsh bowed his head and wept.

His wife crossed to his side and taking him in her arms rocked him as though he was a child.

"Don't take on love, it was my fault I shouldn't have tried to reason with her, you had warned me you thought she was not mentally stable but I did try to explain to her how it was important for us to get home before she informed the police about us. It was all my fault, never in a million years had I wished this to happen all, I wanted was to have the means to save some good people from torture and death at the hands of white fanatics."

Raising her eyes damp with tears to the four men watching she said very quietly "perhaps you had better call the police, but please tell them it was my fault, my husband is entirely innocent."

"Before you do look at this." and with that remark he very carefully opened his wife's blouse and gently drew it off her left shoulder and arm. Running down the left hand side of the torso from her collarbone to just below her left breast was an ugly scar, puckered up as though she had been slashed with a weapon with a serrated edge, which is exactly what had happened.

"The long knife Dorothy Shawcross had wielded had been a long handled bread knife. I managed to stop the bleeding and made a dash to Durham, this is where I had friends who were able to attend to Veronica's wound but as you see it has left her scarred for life.

"So gentlemen that is our story; and yes we did come to see Rosalie's niece on behalf of Aidan, and yes before you ask, he is aware Rosalie is no longer with us. I contacted him as soon as she died and even offered to pay his expenses to come for her memorial service but he explained he was unable to get away at that particular time."

This last remark was made with a degree of bitterness. It was very obvious Dr Walsh's opinion of Aidan Forsythe was much the same as that of Aubrey-Page QC.

"Did you make any money out of your enterprise?" Patrick asked while at the same time not knowing what to expect in reply. But he was surprised to see a flash of anger cross the face of Dr Walsh.

"On the back of the misery these people we cared about. No Mr McKenzie we did not nor did we expect to, it was Mr William Shawcross who made a profit ,we did it and paid for the documents we needed out of a fund we sent up to help those in desperate need to escape. We did not at anytime seek to make money

One more thing which you need to know, we did not know Lindsay or Lucinda had been charged with the murder of her mother. If we had we most certainly would have supplied you with proof it was not her, it was never our intention to let that lovely girl stand trial for a murder she did not commit. It was only after her father told us what had happened which was the reason we came to see her, to check out she was safe. Her father was not very helpful in that respect. He did tell us how he had gone to visit her before her marriage, and had promised at the time that nothing and no-one would keep him away from Lucinda's wedding. But unfortunately he had to present himself in Washington to face charges of fraud and conspiracy to defraud which prevented him attending as promised."

"I agreed to his request and Peter said if I was going so was he." Veronica threw a loving glance at her now very subdued husband, who looked as though his whole world had collapsed around him. "So gentlemen now you have the whole sordid story."

Veronica Walsh sat holding her husband's hand waiting for whatever was going to happen next.

"Will you please answer just one last question? Why are you so anxious to meet with Michael and Fiona Shawcross? They are no relation whatever to the Forsythe family the only connection is through Dorothy."

"Professor Gibson, the only reason is more to do with the boy than his sister. When we visited Aidan he wanted us to find out if Dorothy had been pregnant with the boy when she ran away from Ireland. Had she been expecting a child, this will change things considerably. It means Aidan is father to two children and must make some financial provision, in other words to bring his will up to date."

"My cousin is a very wealthy man, despite his erratic and often wilful lifestyle. His father left him a trust fund, not for his own use, all he has at present is the interest, but in the event of Aidan Forsythe producing offspring the bulk of the money goes to those children upon attaining the age of 25years."

Patrick rose to his feet in a sudden burst of energy, and looking directly at Veronica Walsh asked in a very quiet cold voice, "what's in it for you, and please do not try to evade the question because from where I am sitting, this I believe, is the real reason for your visit."

Dr Peter Walsh looked with total disbelief at the man standing so close to him he could almost feel the anger bouncing off him.

"Gentlemen I have no idea what you mean, I most certainly did not nor do I have any hidden agenda. All I did was to follow up a request from Aidan Forsythe."

"I believe you Dr Walsh but your wife knows what I am referring to, and unless I am very much mistaken it is in her interests if she can prove Aidan actually fathered just the one child but could claim having two. Am I correct in my assumption Mrs Walsh?"

The expression on Veronica Walsh's face was more than enough to confirm Patrick's assumption.

Giving a deep sigh as though it came from the soles of her feet she nodded. "How did you guess Mr McKenzie? Aidan said it was fool proof, all he had to establish was the second child was his knowing in fact he had fathered just the one so far as he knows. The trust would be split into two equal shares, but while his daughter would quite rightly receive one half share, Aidan would keep the other half and split it with me. I would get one third of Aidan's share towards our rescue funds as he so generously explained. That is the only reason I agreed to go along with his plan."

"So! It's just how I imagined; your wretched cousin was more interested in cheating his only child out of her rightful inheritance than her welfare." Patrick almost spit the words out in fury. "I knew there was something smoky about the bloody affair from the start. If I ever lay eyes on that man again I swear to god I will beat him within an inch of his miserable life."

Aubrey crossed to his young brother-in-law.

"No Patrick it will not be necessary to resort to violence, he is not worth risking one single minute of your time. Leave him to me, I will make quite sure the trustees are made of aware of his plans to defraud his daughter and if I am not mistaken they will make sure retribution will be swift and final."

Turning towards Sebastian Aubrey continued; " I think we are more or less done for today, but I would suggest that Dr and Mrs Walsh remain here in this house until tomorrow morning, then we will advise the appropriate authorities who will need to take statements from you both. At this stage I would hazard a guess you will both be charged on several counts. The most serious first being manslaughter. If you wish I will give you the names of a firm of solicitors and they will take it from there. You will in the fullness of time also require the services of a good criminal barrister. Again I can assist you with that. However what I will not do, is to enter into any kind of personal assistance, and as for you Mrs Walsh you can thank your lucky stars I am not likely to be the presiding judge at your trial. Because make no mistake you will go on trial at some stage. I am unable to tell you what the exact charges will be but I am almost certain if found guilty you will face a custodial sentence."

Turning back to Dr Walsh he continued; "You sir were caught in a situation that at times were almost intolerable but it still did not justify the outcome, but thank god it is not me who has to sort out this mess you find yourself in. My advice to you both is to tell the truth, no matter how bad it sounds or who is implicated, and pray for leniency."

Aubrey sat down and the only sound was a quiet weeping. Sebastian rubbed his hand over his face, he felt mentally and physically exhausted.

What a way to start the New Year, all he wanted now was to go back to Cambridge to the stability and warmth of home.

Daniel straightened his back, for the first time he felt his age, dear heavens never in his life had he felt such an aching need to return to normality and his extended family. To hold his relatively new wife close and draw a line under the whole sorry mess.

Patrick excused himself and stepped out of the room to have words with Jim Harris.

After explaining the situation he went in search of Mrs Harris and asked if she would prepare one of the spare bedrooms for Dr and Mrs Walsh who would be staying the night until such time some of his brother's former colleagues would call upon them. He then telephoned Church House and very briefly put Elizabeth in the picture.

"Will you explain to Lucy I will telephone her in about an hour, not to worry it is all over bar the shouting."

For a few minutes he just sat alone with his thoughts then returned to join the others.

CHAPTER 40

Later, once the initial problems re accommodation had been sorted out it was decided in order to save Mrs Harris any unnecessary work they would order a take-away for the evening meal.

Sebastian had in the meantime contacted a former colleague at New Scotland Yard and after giving him a very brief resume of the situation suggested he consult with his senior officer on how best to proceed.

"Dr Peter and Mrs Veronica Walsh are staying here at 27 Bedford Square for the night but I would appreciate someone from whatever department who deals with peculiar cases such as this one collects them a.s.a.p in the morning."

Assuring Sebastian he would speak to the duty officer in charge without further delay, reminded him in view of the seriousness of the possible charges it might be better if the miscreants were interviewed sooner than later.

"It will take the pressure off you Mr McKenzie and also relieve you from the responsibility of making sure they don't attempt to do a runner during the night."

"Thank you, although we here at McKenzie SI take security very seriously and I have already made quite sure this pair will be secure until morning. Although if you or whoever would rather collect earlier than later I will be delighted. However, I want this played low key no *Two's and Blues*, no breaking down of doors and under no circumstances whatever anyone in your establishment notifying the press beforehand. This last request is more important than getting public acclaim for making what can be termed as a very high profile arrest. If you are unable to guarantee any of these conditions don't bother coming, I will bring them along myself tomorrow morning." With these very stringent conditions laid down Sebastian hung up the phone, then went slowly back to the interview room to acquaint the occupants what he had arranged.

The Doctor and his wife listened but did not make any comment. It was as they had more or less expected, and at this point there was little they could say or do to change the situation they had got themselves into. All that remained was to face up to reality and wait.

Daniel said he would wait until they heard from the police, then if the rest of them didn't mind he would go back to Elizabeth and the family.

"I'm beginning to feel my age boys, and I want to go home. If it's OK with you all, I will also take young Michael back with me, he must be just as sick of the whole business as we are, and he has been left more or less on his own for the best part of the day, so I think I will join him upstairs until we know what is happening."

Daniel didn't have to wait long, in less than an hour Jim Harris announced the arrival of Chief Inspector Neville Graham, together with two plain clothes senior police officers.

Introducing his brother and brother-in law, Sebastian invited them into his own personal office where he gave the men a brief resume of all that had transpired during the course of the afternoon and early evening.

"I took the precaution of having everything recorded; the reasons are as follows,

1. At no time were either threats, or coercion made against Dr and Mrs Walsh

2. All the questions put to Dr and Mrs Walsh were to establish the truth in matters appertaining to a member of our family.

3. These answers were given voluntarily by both parties.

We will of course assist you in any way we can, but the same rule applies; no press until such time you find and apprehend the other interested people who cashed in on the procurement of illegal documents for their own questionable profit.

It was almost ten o'clock before the police departed taking the Dr and his wife with them.

Chief Inspector Graham explained the question of bail could not be discussed until the following day, but in view of the severity of the allegations, together with the fact it was a possibility they could skip bail and return to South Africa they both may be detained in custody, but that is to be decided later.

The police contingent left taking the hapless Walsh's with them

Aubrey stretched his arms above his head and giving an almighty yawn apologised to the remaining men. "Sorry about that but I didn't sleep very well last night, and like you I'm sick of the whole sordid business, and I know I sound like one of our children, but I want to go home."

His brothers-in-law grinned in return but it was Patrick who answered.

"You have echoed my sentiments exactly."

"I totally agree with you, and I know Daniel wants to return more or less now."

A slow smile started as an idea seemed to take shape in Aubrey's mind.

"Gentlemen it is too late for any one of us to drive back tonight. We have all had a long and stressful day so may I suggest we leave Daniel's car here and arrange for a hire car take us back home as soon as I can arrange it?

Patrick and Sebastian didn't even stop to consider Aubrey's suggestion. Both nodded then Sebastian said.

"I had better go and tell Daniel and young Michael we are going home in style a.s.a.p."

"Good, so Patrick will you please explain to Mrs Harris we will not be staying over after all and thank Jim Harris for his help while I talk to the car hire company."

While they were waiting for the hire car complete with driver they had all gone up to Patrick and Lucy's apartment where Mrs Harris, despite their protests had prepared a large platter of savoury sandwiches ,together with slices of homemade pork pie and pickle.

"You are not going all that way in the cold and dark on an empty stomach, beside by the time you reach Church House everybody will be in bed, and it's not proper to expect someone to start making supper for you all at that time in the morning."

Mrs Harris went out leaving them to it.

Daniel had had a hard time keeping his face straight during Mrs Harris' little lecture. "She is a kindly soul and I should imagine Mrs Harris more than most, knows all about getting up in the night to tend to male needs."

They all knew Mrs Harris' history before coming as housekeeper for the McKenzie London contingent. Jim Harris as a youngster had been in juvenile trouble on more than one occasion, which had led to several skirmishes with the law in his early to late twenties. He would have ended up a hardened criminal but for the timely intervention of one Detective Inspector McKenzie.

Sebastian had been cornered in an attempted arrest by a bunch of villains, and a young Jim Harris had waded in fists flying and boots kicking at the same time yelling like a proverbial banshee.

"Hang on Mr McKenzie some of my mates are coming but let's give this low life a real lesson in unarmed combat." The rest was history both combatants received a police commendation and Jim came to work for McKenzie SI Ltd as Bodyguard and Butler.

CHAPTER 41

The five men, four of whom were both emotionally and mentally tired arrived back in Cambridge in the wee small hours of 5th January. One day short of Twelfth Night Kate was to remark later in the day.

Before leaving London Aubrey had asked the driver of the hire car if he would care to stay until morning, but the driver while thanking him declined his kind invitation

"I listened to the weather forecast before I came to pick you up sir, and according to the satellite pictures on the television the South East including parts of East Anglia are due for moderate to heavy fall of snow sometime before dawn. So if you don't mind Sir I will drop you off and make tracks for home a.s.a.p."

However the promised snow had not yet put in appearance which made it an un- eventful journey back to Church House in record time.

The only light in evidence was the drive was lit with the Christmas Lights and the big lamp over the front door made a very welcome sight.

The front door opened and waiting to welcome the men home was Josephine.

Holding out her hands she welcomed them each with a hug and a kiss.

Putting his arm round his wife's shoulders Aubrey drew her close to his side.

"You should be in bed sweetheart we could have seen to ourselves for one night."

"Yes of course you could but I couldn't sleep. I went up to bed just after eleven but all I did was watch the clock go round. But enough chit chat let me make you all something to eat or a warm drink then it's off to bed for all of you. We can talk later when we are all fresh and able to take on board all you have to tell us."

As they followed Josephine into the family parlour none of the men were at all surprised to find the other ladies of the household waiting for them.

"Lucy." Patrick closed the room in two strides, "darling you should have stayed in bed; you must rest as much as possible." Putting his arms around his wife Patrick drew her close.

"Hush love, I'm not some delicate little flower, just another lady who is expecting a baby, but tell me are you OK you sounded stressed when you telephoned earlier."

"As Aubrey has just said we will have a family get together later on today and bring you all up to date."

Stifling a large yawn Daniel simply just held on to Elizabeth truly thankful to be home

Christina had waited until her Brothers-in-law and Step Papa -in-Law had greeted Elizabeth before she joined her husband to welcome him back into the family fold.

"Feeling a familiar frisson just behind him Sebastian turned into the loving embrace of his wife.

"My Love lets go up now, you look as though you have had a stressful day and evening and it's time to rest." Turning to the rest of the inhabitants in the room she said; "Good night everybody but I am now taking my husband to bed, it is time for him to have some quality time with me. We have not had a lot of personal time together over this holiday and I am going to make sure he has at least eight hours rest, starting from now."

So once again bidding the rest of the tribe goodnight she took her beloved Sebastian to bed.

Once inside their bedroom she lost no time in turning on the shower, and laying out warm towels prior to getting him into bed.

Showered, and warm, Sebastian lost no time in climbing into bed beside the love of his life.

"Give me a cuddle woman." he said turning to take her into his arms."Do you know this is the third time I have been away from you at bedtime, even when the babies arrived I was with you all the time more or less until you came home, and my darling it is going to be the last. I don't like being away from you during the night or even just part of the night. Christina have I told you how very much I love and treasure you lately?"

Holding her man close Christina simply kissed him and held him to her as he closed his eyes and drifted off, safe in the knowledge of loving and been loved.

CHAPTER 42

The promised snow had not yet materialized but it was just short of being bitter cold. So Miriam had corralled all the children and with the help of Ava Blossom planned to take the children into Cambridge to see the pretty lights before they all were taken down.

This left the respective Daddies and Grandpa to regale the rest of the family with the dramatic events of the previous day.

The meeting was to be held in what was Christopher's room, so he was brought into the loop without causing him too much stress.

As the rest of the family members including Michael and Fiona took their places more than one adult had reason to smile.

Tucked up in the crook of his uncle's arm was one Frederick McKenzie Page.

"Miriam and Ava have taken the other children into Cambridge but Freddie is too young as yet to enjoy that particular outing so his uncle Christopher suggested he would give his youngest nephew a cuddle while he listens to your latest adventures." Freddie's mother explained with a huge grin, at the same time thinking how holding the small child suited him.

It's about time he settled down and had a child of his own to cuddle thought Heather as she took a seat near Christopher. Hopefully if she was correct in her assumptions about a certain nanny and Christopher that might just happen for next Christmas. All she could do for the present was to pray, as she sat back waiting for Sebastian to commence.

"I think we are all familiar with the origins of the reasons for the enquiry into the terrible and tragic happening to Lucy before she became a member of this family, so I won't go over those details again. However the two traumatic events did have a bearing on each other as we first thought, but not connected in the actual deed.

So to be as brief as possible I will explain how the second was indirectly a result of the first."

Sebastian told how Mrs Walsh had read of the terrible assault on the then Lindsay Shawcross, together with photographs of the injured young woman showing her before and after the attack.

This led to the blackmail of Lindsay's mother Dorothy and her step father William Shawcross. Mrs Walsh did not want money, she wanted documents to help smuggle one of their friends out of South Africa to the UK.

However after Mr Shawcross did as he was asked, Mrs Walsh continued to request more. But someone else also wanted in on the act. This person was part of a larger group, who wanted access to same kind of documents but not for humane reasons, they saw it as a way to make a lot of money."

"So I am right in suggesting it was someone in this group Caroline Daly and me had trouble with in the North East." queried Christopher in a quiet voice.

Heather rose and sat on the edge of his bed and took a hold of his hand as though to comfort him.

"More than likely." his brother said before continuing

"But Mrs Shawcross and her husband were getting frightened, and Mr Shawcross decided they were going to the police to confess what they had been doing, they wanted out.

So the final time Mrs Walsh contacted Dorothy Shawcross, Dr Walsh went with his wife to the Shawcross household to plead with them at least wait five days giving them, the Walsh's time to return to South Africa."

Sebastian continued giving the listeners an edited account of that terrible night when Dorothy Shawcross had lost her life.

"At this time we are not is a position to make any comment as to who was to blame for Dorothy's death but what is absolutely clear is my beautiful and very brave Lucy was not in any way responsible for the murder of her mother." this last statement was made by a very emotional Patrick.

Lucy just sat as Patrick held her close.

At that precise moment she was not quite sure what she felt, but one thing she was absolutely certain of was the love she had for all those present, her very own extended family. Placing one hand into Patrick's and the other on her tummy she spoke to them all in a quiet but confident voice.

"In less than six months we, Patrick and me are going to become parents, the very best parents as humanely possible. Another child to add to the McKenzie family tree and as this family tree will increase over the years to come, I will make a promise to you all, especially my beloved Patrick; I will never cease to be grateful for your loving support so long as I shall live."

More than one person in that room felt more than emotional but just as one or two were wiping their eyes a mini tornado erupted into the room, followed by Ava and Miriam.

"We are back and its starting snow, can we build a snowman?" This statement was made by Sebastian's twin boys all in one breath, followed by the smallest boy, Aubrey's Oliver.

"Daddy, I seed snow."

Swinging his son up into his arms Aubrey nuzzled his face into his little son's neck. "As soon as we have enough to build a snowman we will play, but how about you tell your mummy and me what you saw when you went to Cambridge?."

Looking directly into his daddy's eyes Oliver put his baby arms round his neck saying "lots of pretty lights, but I love you best." Then almost at once turned to see his little brother being cuddled up with his Uncle Christopher asked. "Is Unca Christopher a daddy like you?"

Ava Blossom hearing what Oliver said saw a look of what? Could it be longing she couldn't be sure but she did know how to get rid of it. Letting her eyes rest on the man in bed with young Freddie she replied to Oliver's question but kept her gaze on Christopher as she spoke. "Not yet darling but I'm sure that can be arranged."

Daniel and Elizabeth were to remark later in the privacy of their room.

"Do you think what I am thinking Daniel? Has Charles Blossom's sister got designs on my youngest son?"

"From where I was standing I would say she most certainly has." replied Daniel. "It's my guess we are going have another pair entering into holy matrimony sooner than later, but don't get your hopes just yet."

Daniel was correct in the matter of another wedding in the family but, both he and Elizabeth were wrong in their assumption of their son's choice for his bride to be.

At the same time as Ava replied to Oliver's question Miriam came into the room followed by Great Aunt Grace. Both ladies heard Ava's answer directed at Christopher.

Keeping her expression from showing hurt or distress, Miriam stepped forward to collect the little child from his uncle.

Christopher had spent a lot of time in the nursery since his abrupt break with Sybil Buchanan. Playing with his sister's children gave him a sense of peace and contentment he had not realised he was looking for, together with the added bonus of getting to know Miriam Khan.

Over the past several of months he had enjoyed talking to Miriam about all manner of subjects, from art to music, books and travel. One evening he had popped into the nursery to kiss his nephews goodnight when he heard Miriam singing a familiar nursery rhyme not in English but in its original French.

"When I first came to Pipers Gate, Heather used to sing the same song to me but in English," commented Christopher as he joined in.

Smiling at her employer's brother she admitted to being fluent is several European languages.

"Yet you are content to being a Nanny always looking after other people's children."

"I always wanted to have a career involving children, this is not quite what I had in mind when I was in my mid teens, but circumstances over which I had little control prevented me completing my education."

She turned away from him but not before he saw a look of incredible sadness in her eyes. Not knowing the reason for her reaction Christopher was shaken by his response to this woman, not only was she highly intelligent and very lovely, with what he would describe later to his mother, as a timeless beauty which would last through all the stages of her life. It was very evident she loved the children very much. Much the same as Heather had with him and his siblings. He would very much like to get to know this self possessed lady better, no, a whole lot better.

Before leaving he put his hand very carefully on her arm asking; "If you can spare the time will you come for walk with me, or perhaps I can join you when you take the little ones for a walk.

So over a period time they found they both enjoyed each other's company. After they discovered they had much in common Miriam allowed herself to dream.

Upon hearing Ava Blossom's response, Miriam, keeping slight smile on her face took step towards Christopher's bed in order to take Freddie back to the nursery.

Dame Grace Drummond had also taken on board the suggestion made indirectly to her great nephew, she too had seen his brilliant smile, but it had not been directed at one Miss Ava Blossom as everybody thought, but the smile was directed slightly to the left of Ava's right shoulder, straight to the young nanny who was standing directly in front of Grace.

With a beaming smile Grace stepped in front of Miriam, while at the same time saying;-

" Let me take him, it is high time this young man got to know his Great, Great, Aunty Grace." Matching actions to words she swooped down and bending towards Christopher gently took the child from his arms into her own. Placing her face close to her nephew's ear whispered. "If you are lucky and she accepts you, you will have got yourself someone very, very, special, but tread carefully don't try to rush her." Giving him a quick kiss she joined Miriam in the doorway. "Do you mind if I come up to the nursery with you? It's a long time since I was involved with someone so young."

As Grace was leaving Sebastian heard his Great Aunt give a very slight gasp.

Freddie was looking up into the face looking down at him with a tiny frown which would have indicated he was about cry, but not this time. Freddie gazed up at the person holding him so carefully with a slightly puzzled look in his eyes as though he recognised her. Reaching up, his placed his small hand on her sleeve. Grace gazed down at the child and her eyes were bright with tears.

Sebastian held his breath what was going on here? His question was answered in less than one second.

Grace Drummond stood perfectly still, then speaking very quietly said; " John, my darling boy I waited so long for you, I knew you would come back some day, all I ask will you wait for me?"

When Sebastian related the strange conversation his Great Aunt had with Josephine's infant son to Christina she asked the all important question.

"Was John a son or perhaps a grandson?"

"Neither, he was her first and only true love. My mother told me Grace had fallen deeply in love with a local young man but her father sent him away, he considered he was not good enough for his only daughter."

"Why was he considered not suitable?"

"For starters he was not the same class as his daughter, plus had little money as a jobbing builder. But John Clayton did not remain a builder in that respect, instead he turned his hand to renovation and design, renovating mostly buildings left to fall into wilful disrepair. In later years he made a fortune in repairing and restoring bomb damaged properties. His company was always in demand. John Clayton was a byword in that particular branch of the industry. His honesty and attention to detail was phenomenal, but most of all his honesty. He was as straight as a die.

Grace met up with him in February 1959 quite by chance. She had contacted his company for advice about installing central heating in her grade two listed house. John Clayton came himself to satisfy his curiosity. The name Drummond rang a distant bell, so he came to Long Melford and never left. They lived together for just over nine very happy years then John died quite suddenly.

Grandpa Drummond went with Ma to the funeral and found out the reason they had not married. John already had a wife but the only thing she was interested in was John's money. That is why she wouldn't divorce him, besides it gave her a certain status being able to claim him as her husband."

"So you think she is," Christina didn't voice the word which had come to mind.

"No love she most certainly is not losing her marbles and I don't think it is actually Freddie's features, it is more likely the way he looks at her. I think it's his sometimes solemn scrutiny when he is sure he knows you, you get that smile that seems to make his eyes dance; it's uncanny."

"Yes I know what you mean and I agree for one so young, I find it a bit strange. It doesn't happen very often, in fact I would say rarely. My goodness it makes you wonder if such a thing as reincarnation does really exist."

Taking his wife in his arms Sebastian responded to her question.

"Oh yes my darling it does, remember when I came to Mayfield Row that very first time and I comforted you in the kitchen, we recognised each other. At first you didn't believe we knew each other from another time, but I never doubted for a single minute you belonged to me."

Placing her arms around him she drew him to closer to her. "My love if what you are suggesting is correct, John Clayton is now here, waiting for Grace to come back sometime in the future?"

Sebastian resting his head against his wife's replied in a low voice, "I would like to think so, to have a fulfilled and happy marriage as we have."

Dropping a swift kiss on Christina's head Sebastian said, "Let's go and find our boys, its family play time."